D1344015

Pat Moon

Hodder
Children's
Books

a division of Hodder Headline Limited

With thanks to:

Sam, for nagging me into writing this book, and for the title

*Vron Jones and Annie James of The King's School,
Ottery St. Mary, Devon for their help, and their students
for their comments, ideas and feedback.*

*Rob Pattman of Birkbeck College, The University of London, for
his study on Emergent Masculinities: 11- to 14-year-old boys.*

Text copyright © 2001 Pat Moon
First published in Great Britain in 2001 by Hodder Children's Books

A Catalogue record for this book is available from
the British Library

ISBN 0 340 80520 X

Typeset by Avon Dataset Ltd, Bidford-on-Avon, Warks

Printed and bound in Great Britain by
The Guernsey Press Co. Ltd, Channel Isles

Hodder Children's Books
a division of Hodder Headline Ltd
338 Euston Road
London NW1 3BH

MONDAY

08.05 *Waiting for the school bus*

Denise and Mel are shrieking and laughing at something Sonya's reading out from a magazine. They're Year Nine, same as me. They're trying to get some attention from Stuart Doyle and Tony Sharples – but Doyle mainly.

I can't believe some of the things she's reading out – about sex and stuff. If boys do that, girls have a go at you: they tell you you're totally sex-obsessed or perverted. Yet Sonya and her mates are always on about it. It's embarrassing, especially when you're on your own. I try to keep well away, but not look geeky – as if I know more than they think I know. I've been practising in the mirror. They just love winding you up, so you have to give as good as you get. You can't even get a haircut without getting a running commentary and piss-taking for days afterwards.

I've got this stupid crazy hair anyway, it grows in all directions. My Uncle Edwin had it too. I've got a couple of photos of him. One when he was just a bit older than me, taken in 1914, just before he set off to France to fight the Germans. He's in his army uniform. His hair's been cropped by the regimental barber, but it still manages to look like a black hedgehog sitting on his head. I've got the same mouth as him too. That's who I'm named after. *Great-great* Uncle Edwin to be exact, except I'm Ed for short. I hate being called Edwin. I looked it up in a book once – it means wine-drinking friend. Funny sort of name to give to a little baby.

It's kind of interesting how kids always keep to their own little territories here. The new Year Sevens in a huddle near the lamppost, ear-wigging every word but trying to look like they're not. Sonya and her mates leaning against the wall, flashing looks at Doyle and Sharples.

The big mistake is to be fooled by Sonya's little-girl voice, baby-blue eyes and long blond hair. She can be scary. Even Mel, who's big, loud and pushy, does exactly what Sonya tells her. Denise *used* to be Sonya's best friend, but she got moved into a different class last term. Now Sonya enjoys playing them off against each other. Denise has this thick dark hair – she keeps tossing it back and running her fingers through it. She thinks this is dead sexy. But I think it's really annoying, especially when you sit behind her in Maths and keep getting mouthfuls of it.

Stuart Doyle and Tony Sharples are playing it all cool and mature. Like they're not interested in all the attention, now that they're super-beings in the Sixth Form and all. As if they're a different species because they don't have to wear the uniform any more. But Sharples is enjoying every minute of it. He's got this smug grin and his eyes keep darting over at them. Doyle's leaning against the lamppost, staring into space, like it's all beneath him – though making sure that they get the benefit of his perfect profile. He's very proud of his profile is Doyle, and his hair. I know this because I caught him in the bogs once, standing in front of the mirror, studying himself from every angle, lovingly smoothing his golden locks.

Look at that gear he's wearing. Very nice. That didn't come from Top Man did it? Must have cost a packet. His parents run the George Hotel – I remember my sister Ellie going there with the rest of her class for his birthday party a few years back. He thinks a lot of himself, he really does.

Here comes Lester, on the other side of the road, taking his time, looking over his shoulder for the bus. *Don't hurry*, I tell him in my head. Not that he needs telling.

Sonya's started reading out a letter from the magazine now. '*Is my boyfriend gay?*' she reads. '*He says he loves me but he doesn't like kissing me! He's always reading my magazines. And I found a magazine under his bed – full of hunky pin-up men. Should I confront him?*'

'Chuck him, more like!' screams Mel. They collapse into shrieks of laughter.

Lester's crossing over. He waits, watching for the bus,

keeping his distance as always. I see Sharples watching him. He's muttering something into Doyle's ear – has to stretch a bit to reach. Doyle's tall, athletic-looking, but Sharples is short and chunky. Slowly, Doyle peels himself from the lamppost. Together they move towards Lester . . .

They've stopped right in front of him. I groan inside. Lester's acting like they're not there, staring down at his feet. Lester's practically the same height as Doyle, but looks smaller somehow. The girls are all eyes now. Doyle peers into Lester's face.

'Tell me something, Lester,' he says, in this fake serious way. 'Do you or do you not enjoy kissing?'

Hoots and yells from Sonya's group. I don't want to watch this.

'Girls, he means,' smirks Tony Sharples. 'Do you enjoy kissing *girls*?'

Lester's not saying anything. He never does.

'And furthermore, have you, at any time, read girls' magazines?' Doyle asks.

I'm thinking, *Don't ask ME! Plee-ea-se don't ask me*. I mean, I read my sister's magazines all the time. I focus my attention on to a piece of chewing gum stuck to the pavement.

'Hello? Hello? Anyone there?' jokes Sharples, peering up into Lester's face (Lester's taller than him).

'OK. Question Number Three,' says Doyle. 'Do you by any chance keep magazines of hunky male pin-ups under your bed? Come on, now. Don't be shy. We won't tell anyone.'

The girls are bent double over this.

'Perhaps he's got his name mixed up,' Denise screeches. 'Are you sure you're Lester Carroll and not Carol Lester?'

They're really getting off on it. Some kids flash glances towards Lester, then act like it's nothing to do with them. Me included.

Lester looks white. Really white. Just stands there, looking down. Waiting for them to leave him alone. He's got very white skin anyway, and this silvery hair, and he's even skinnier than me. But it looks like all his blood has drained out.

It makes me want to puke, the pleasure they're getting from it. What makes it worse is that Lester used to be my best mate – inseparable we were. Until he let me down. Got to admit, some of the best times I ever had were with Lester. Not that I'd go round telling this to anyone. He could be so funny sometimes. Really, really funny. You see, Lester's an original. He really is . . . But it's not too smart being an original. You get picked on. It's best to merge with the crowd. Go with the flow. I'm not saying he *is* gay. Maybe he is. Maybe he isn't. I never really thought about it till kids started saying it. Wouldn't bother me if anyone's gay or not. Better than being a two-faced arsehole, like Doyle. Hey, that's quite funny. I've got this cartoon picture in my head. Stuart Doyle, the two-faced arsehole.

At ruddy last – the bus. I sit next to Ryan as usual. Doyle and Sharples join their mate Christos Zimmer at the back of the bus. Lester always sits on his own. But this time Sonya and her friends crowd into the seat behind him. I know – I just know – they haven't finished with him.

Mel's got this spray bottle of perfume which they're passing round and trying out. Then Denise jumps up, leans over the seat and gives Lester a dousing. Suddenly he comes alive, ducking and diving. But he doesn't stand a chance. It goes all over him. The bus stinks. Kids at the front are turning round. Grinning heads pop up over seats to see what it's all about. The driver's yelling at us to sit down and stop all the noise. Some, Ryan included, think it's a big joke. Others look away. They don't want to get involved. Some new kids, all neat in their shiny shoes and stiff blazers, are looking a bit unsure and nervous.

It settles down. But I can see Mel and Sonya writing little notes, rolling them into balls and tossing them over the headrest at Lester. Lester sits there, face turned to the window, ignoring this snowstorm of little paper balls bouncing on his head. They're really giving him the works this morning. They'll be laughing and joking about it later, telling Brett, Clive and Jason, their mates. There's hardly a day without that crowd giving Lester some aggravation. I don't know how he puts up with it.

We turn into the school car park. What's Mel doing now? She's plonked herself next to Lester. She's a big girl is Mel. She'll be hard to budge.

I get up – Ryan grabs my arm. 'Hang about – I wanna see what happens.'

I leave him there and wait outside. The driver's shouting to everyone hurry up and get off. Ryan and some others clamber out, followed by Tony Sharples, Christos Zimmer and the three girls. They wait. Where's Stuart Doyle, then? Lester's next, head down – can't see his face. And Doyle's right behind him. Lester tries to move off but Doyle glides in front, peers into his face and says, all maternal like, 'Oh dear. Is that a tear I see? We're not going to *cry* are we? We can't have that.'

'Aaah – poor little thing!' mocks Sonya.

Groups of kids stand watching. Loads of stupid grinning faces.

Doyle's making it up – all this tear stuff! He can't get to Lester – that's what he can't take. No one can get to him. Not really. Not to the inside. I know Lester better than anyone. I've never seen him cry. Not even when he shot over the handlebars of my bike and landed on a gatepost. Thirty-one stitches he needed in his leg. Not even when Brett and his mates cornered him in the showers and . . .

Doyle's going *sniff, sniff* at him. 'God! Lester!' He fans the air with his hands. 'You stink like a tart!'

Loads of kids find this funny.

Lester stands, staring down, waiting patiently for Doyle to let him pass. I don't want to see any more of this. I'm out of here . . . oh, no . . . plee-ease – no! I don't want to see this! Looks like Lester *is* crying. Why now? He's taken worse than this before. A big drip hanging from his nose – why doesn't he wipe it way – why doesn't he go? Just standing there like a dummy. Go, Lester! Just go! Can't take my eyes off that drip – the total humiliation of that drip. It falls on to his jacket. Snot's running from his nose . . .

Someone sniggers. Suddenly Doyle seems to lose interest. He's wandering off – Sharples and Zimmer alongside. Inside my head, a switch flips. And I'm hearing my voice calling to Doyle's back, 'You think you're so big, don't you! Well the only big thing about you is your mouth! It certainly isn't your brain! Because your brain is this big! See?'

A wave of laughter – as Doyle turns to see me demonstrating the size of his brain. With my finger and thumb, as if I'm holding a pea.

Hey! I've done the right thing! Everyone's on my side! They're laughing! Well, OK, not Doyle and his mates. It's electric.

I catch Lester looking at me. For a millisecond our eyes make contact. Doyle hasn't moved. He stands, staring at me from under his eyelashes. Then he starts to walk back towards me.

Sweaty panic washes over me. Hell's bells – what have I done? What have I done . . . He's stopped right in front of me – up close – staring at me with those freaky blue eyes of his. My insides are doing bungee jumps. He just stares and stares. My eyes are getting watery trying not to blink. It's like a game he's playing with me.

'You don't scare me.' It comes out of my mouth like a croak.

He smiles and shakes his head like I'm some sort of saddo.

I want to disappear – to walk away. I feel everyone's eyes on me, waiting for something to happen. He doesn't move a muscle. Just waits. But I'm not going to walk or look away – I won't, I won't, I won't! I hate him . . .

He's smiling – why's he smiling? He puts his face up close. I can smell his toothpaste.

'OK, you've got till Friday,' he hisses in my ear. 'Four whole days – enjoy them. Then we'll arrange a little meeting – just you and me. And we'll see if I scare you or not. I'll let you know the time and place.'

He turns to go, then smirks, 'If you can't make it – no worries. Just have to make another appointment, won't we?'

He strolls away.

'Bloody hell, Ed!' Ryan breathes into my neck. He's standing right behind me, acting invisible. 'You've just committed suicide.'

'What was all that about?' says someone.

Everyone is looking at me. I see my other mates, Dougie and Carl, pushing their way towards me. I can't see Lester – he's vanished.

'Woo-hoo! Are you stupid or something?' It's Denise.

'So what was Doyle saying to you, then?' demands Sonya. 'Go on – tell us!'

I tell her to get lost.

Sonya smirks. 'You're the one who ought to get lost, 'cos Doyle's never gonna let you get away with that. You are one sad person – you really are.'

'Yeah – and you're gonna be even sadder!' adds Mel as they stalk off, laughing.

'He's gonna do you!' shouts a small freckly kid with glasses. Kids laugh.

Carl does his big bear act and growls at them to scram. Carl can do that. He gets a lot of respect. He's big and black and has this moustache if he forgets to shave. Also he has a girlfriend in Year Ten. There aren't many girls who'd go out with a boy younger than them – but there're loads lining up for Carl. He passes for eighteen, easy. Unlike me. OK, I'm five-six and a half, but so skinny I have to pad myself out with layers of T-shirts just to look normal.

Carl stares down at me. 'Are you crazy? Man! What did you do that for!'

'You are not gonna believe what Ed told Doyle there,' says Ryan shaking his head.

'You are not gonna believe it . . .'

People are still hanging around, all eyes and flapping ears. I head for some space. I can't think. I don't want to think. They catch me up.

'So what was going on there?' asks Carl.

Ryan blurts, 'Wanna know what Ed just told Doyle? He only told him, "*You don't scare me!*" ' He puts on this stupid gangster voice.

Carl stares at me. 'You told him *what?*'

'And there's going to be a fight or something! Doyle said, "*OK – you've got four days till Friday – then it's just you and me – and we'll see if I scare you or not!*" ' He blinks at me. 'Ed – you – are – gonna – get – pulped!' He jiggles from foot to foot. It really annoys me the way he can't keep still.

'Have you got a death wish or something?' squeals Dougie. 'Why'd you do that!'

'Am I allowed I speak?' I ask.

They stand waiting. *Why* did *I do that?* I'm thinking. I shrug. 'I dunno. It just made me mad – the way Doyle gets pleasure from making people look stupid! All of them – having a go. You didn't see all of it . . .'

I fill them in a bit about the stuff that happened at the bus stop and on the bus.

Dougie gawps at me. 'So, you put your head on the line for Lester?'

Dougie and Carl are related. Second cousins or something, but they're not alike. Dougie's nowhere like

Carl's build and he's a bit of a fusser, especially over the way he dresses and having all the right gear.

'I was watching Doyle's face,' says Ryan. 'He was acting cool but he was really mad. I could see his mind working out what to do to you. He was enjoying it – specially when he added that bit about, "*If you can't make it, no worries – we'll make another appointment.*" That was to make sure you turn up. There's no way out, Ed.'

I'm feeling like I'm not really here. Like it's a bad dream and I'll wake up in a sec.

'But Doyle didn't say anything about a *fight*,' I tell them, trying to stop the panic inside. 'He said something about Friday and just me and him. I mean – he's just trying to put the frighteners on me, isn't he?'

'Oh, yeah?' nods Carl. 'Like on Friday he's gonna shake your hand and you become buddies for life? Because no one else stands up to him – and he respects someone who does? What planet are you from?'

The bell goes. We make our way towards school. Mel's screeching laugh reaches us. I can see the three girls with Brett and Clive and Jason, looking over in this direction. No prizes for guessing what they're talking about. Hope Lester's skived off or they'll be giving him even more grief. Lester-baiting is their hobby.

'It's stupid getting done for Lester. He asks for it,' Ryan mutters. 'You're going to get pulped – no mistake.'

'No he isn't,' says Dougie.

I look at Dougie. 'I'm not?'

Dougie shrugs. 'Seriously, it isn't Doyle's style is it? He doesn't go round beating people up, does he? He's not a thug. He's smart.' He stares at me. 'Don't you get it? He wants to keep you guessing – not knowing what's going to happen. Then he'll make you look small, like he did Lester.'

'Yeah,' agrees Ryan. 'Mental torture, that is – worse than being beaten up.' He shakes his head at me. 'Worse than a punch in the goolies, that is.'

'Oh thanks, Ryan. That's really made me feel better. Thanks a lot.'

Carl says, 'All we're saying is you are going to need all the help you can get.'

'Hey, I don't want no trouble,' says Dougie.

'Doyle must have something in mind for Friday,' Ryan rattles on. 'Why else would he say, "*We'll meet up – just you and me*"? Eh? I bet—'

'Ryan,' Carl interrupts. 'Shut up.'

'How long d'you reckon I was standing there with Doyle?' I ask Dougie as we head into school.

He shrugs. 'Dunno – fifty, sixty seconds at the most.'

Is that all? Felt like for ever. This isn't real. I didn't do that. I don't do stuff like that. I need the bog. Urgently.

■

Sitting in the cubicle staring down at my trousers round my ankles. Second bell goes. Gonna be late. Ha-ha.

That's funny – really funny. Worried about being late?
On my way out I catch sight of myself in the mirror.
Stop frowning. Make out like you're not bothered. Act
cool. No – *cool*, I said, not bonkers.

■

In the classroom Sonya and Mel have a crowd round
them. Denise and the others are in different classes. The
six of them were split up because of some trouble they
caused last year.

I hear Sonya's voice. '. . . *then he says, "Lester – do you
or do you not enjoy kissing girls"*'!'

Big laughs. Not from everyone. Clare, Meera, Lauren
and Jasmine sit at their table, keeping to themselves.
But they're listening all right. Lester used to hang around
with them all the time. Until certain people started
calling him a girl and giving him a hard time.

Sonya spots me. 'Hey – look! It's Terminator Three!'
More laughs. Now I'm surrounded.

'You really did that!' says Paul Young. 'What was it
again? "*Your brain's only this big*"!' He holds up his finger
and thumb. 'I'd start praying if I was you.'

Mel grabs my arm, holds it up and squeezes my
biceps. 'Nah! Look! Pure muscle!'

Ha, ha, ha. So funny.

'Get lost, Mel!' I shake her off.

'Oooo! A hard man,' she squeals.

'Yeah – but what did Doyle say to you, Ed?' smiles Sonya. 'We all know he said something. So why aren't you telling, eh? Is it 'cos you're scaredy-waredy, then?'

Everyone's looking at me. I feel the sweat break out under my arms. I take my time walking to my table. What can I say? Think! Think of something to say! Something to take the pressure off . . . I dump my bag, sit down and stretch out. Act like Mr Cool – not Mr Sweaty.

Carl, sitting on his table, feet on a chair, leans forward on his arms; big, watchful, saying nothing. Dougie scrubs away at some mark on his trainer. Ryan grins and fidgets.

'Sonya,' I say. 'You really ought to be in *The Guinness Book of Records*. Honest. Under BIG MOUTHS.'

Hoots and howls. I relax a tiny bit.

'Look who's talking! All mouth and no trousers, you!' Sonia sneers and flounces back to Mel.

'Yeah, probably not a lot inside his trousers, either!' Mel squawks.

'Unless you wanna prove otherwise, Ed!' Sonya cackles.

Jeers from kids who think this is hilarious.

'It's stupid,' announces Louise Lowe to no one in particular. 'Typical boy stuff. Trying to act hard.'

Mr Hargreaves bursts in. Late as usual. The bell for first period goes. Everyone returns to their tables. He tells Dougie to take off his parka, runs his eyes round the room. 'Lester Carroll absent. Anyone else?' He never bothers to call the register. 'Right, you lot – get a move on or you'll be late.'

09.25 Geography

'Here are two maps, both of the town of Hambourne,' says Mrs Kepple, pointing to the projector screen. 'One dated 1901, the other 1990. I want you to study both these maps and list the changes that took place between those times. Use your rough books.'

He's going to pulp you, no mistake. Ryan's voice plays in my head. I see my battered body on the ground, surrounded by jeering faces.

No, Dougie's right, I try telling myself. Doyle doesn't go round beating people up. He'll just make me look small. DON'T THINK ABOUT IT! DON'T THINK ABOUT IT! Look at the maps. Look – Hambourne had a railway station in 1901, but it had gone by 1990. Wow, that's interesting – not. OK, what else?

But I'm back in the car park again. Calling out to Doyle and demonstrating the size of his brain. I keep seeing Lester's face too – when he looked at me. As clear as anything. What was he trying to tell me? *A bit late, aren't you? What about all those other times with Brett and his mates? Why didn't you say something then? All those times in the showers? The school field trip? Remember?* Yeah. Loads of times. Loads of little tortures.

There's a loud ringing in my ears. I'm back in Geography. It's the bell for morning break.

10.35 Break

As we make for the playground, Dougie says, 'I need the bog.'

Kids keep coming up to me. News has travelled fast. There can't have been more than twenty in the car park who saw what happened. Suddenly, I'm popular.

'Hey – what was Stuart Doyle saying to you after you made him look a jerk?' asks someone.

'You're dead!' answers another. They laugh.

'Doyle's OK. He hasn't done you any harm, has he?' says a kid with a mouthful of jammy dodger.

'Not yet,' Ryan mutters.

I see Dougie making his way back towards us. I know by the way he's hurrying that something's wrong. Why's he holding his jacket in front of himself, like that?

'Those bastards! Those bastards! Those flicking pigs!' he's cursing. 'Look! Look! Look what they done to me! They're sick!' He's really shaken up.

His trousers look like he's wet himself.

He glares at me. 'They pissed on me! Two of them held me – and the other pissed on me!'

'See what you done?' says Ryan. 'See what you done!'

'Who was it?' grunts Carl.

'Dunno! There were three of them – Year Elevens,

I think!' Dougie stares down at his trainers. They're squelching.

'Fifty-nine quid they cost me! Fifty-nine quid! They're sick! They're really sick!' He's almost crying. 'One minute I'm coming out the door – the next I'm shoved against the wall – and then—'

From behind us comes a knocking sound. We turn and look up. Framed behind the glass of the Sixth-Form common-room window are the shadowy smiling faces of Doyle, Sharples and Zimmer. Then they're gone. As if they were never there.

'Jeez,' sighs Carl, looking at me.

'You've really started something now, Ed!' puffs Ryan.

Dougie glares at me. 'Thanks, Ed! Thanks a lot! I don't want no part of this. I stink. I'm going home!'

We watch him stride towards the school gates. And the bell tells us it's the end of break.

'Bloody hell, bloody hell,' mutters Ryan, over and over as we head into school.

'They think they're above everyone else. That's what I really hate,' says Carl. 'They really think they're above us.'

10.45 Double English

I'm in a different set to Carl and Ryan. I drop into my usual seat next to Andrew Paisley.

'You're mad, you are,' he mutters.

'Quiet!' It's Mr Day.

He got Dougie. Crafty, really crafty – that's Doyle's style all right. Doyle's setting them against me, isn't he?

'Gavin, Lauren – pass these books round.'

Dougie's mad at me. Ryan's scared.

'Now, last lesson we looked at Act One, Scene Three of *The Merchant of Venice* – so you'll be able to tell me all about it. Won't you?'

What about Carl? He didn't say much did he?

'Now here, if I remember correctly, Ali Patel gave a stunning performance as the handsome Bassanio.' A few guffaws. 'And Glenn Barnes brought the house down as a rather over-the-top Shylock.' A slow hand clap.

'*See what you've started*!' Ryan's voice echoes in my head. But I didn't start anything, did I? It started way back. What's he think? I'm some sort of hari-kiri, kamikaze suicide pilot or something? All I wanted was to stop it.

'Close your eyes,' says Mr Day. 'Get a picture in your head of Shylock. See Shylock's face. What do you think he looks like?'

All I get is a picture of Stuart Doyle. Those freaky blue eyes of his stare back at me. I see his thick blond hair. Dougie's right. He's not a thug. He's smart. And yeah, he's very good-looking. Even I have to admit that. He's got these sculptured cheekbones. If I was a girl – and I'm not – I'd probably think he was the best-looking guy I'd ever seen. And his brain is not, like I demonstrated, that small. He's one of the clever kids who got a million starred As in GCSEs last term. One of the others is my sister, Ellie.

Someone on the table behind me gives me a shove. I look up to see Mr Day leaning over my table.

'Are you with us, Mr Tully? The question was, what do we know about Shylock?'

'Er . . . he's a Jew, Mr Day.'

'Oh, well done!' he announces to the class. 'My efforts have not been wasted – something *has* sunk into that head of yours!

'When this play was first staged,' Mr Day goes on, 'somewhere around the year 1600, Shylock would, almost certainly, have been played as a buffoon . . .'

I see Stuart Doyle standing on a stage. The school stage – last week's whole school assembly. Doyle's not a buffoon. He puts on an act though. He uses this easy-going smooth style. Real oozy and smarmy. Loads of teachers are fooled by it. Especially Mr Barraclough, Head of PE. And Mr Grimshaw, Head of School. I can see him announcing that the over-sixteens football team, '. . . *has yet again won the latest match – thanks to the coaching and leadership of Mr Barraclough and team captain, Stuart Doyle.*'

Doyle faking a humble shrug – then reading his match report, '. . . *and thanks to a truly spectacular half-volley from Simon Jenks – get his autograph now folks, it'll be valuable one day,*' (pause for laughter) – '*finished with seconds to spare, to a two-one victory for Heathlands High!*'

Cheers and applause. Mr Barraclough steps forward. '*I think I ought to point out that the other goal was scored by none other than Stuart Doyle himself.*' More cheers.

They think the sun shines out of his jockstrap, they really do. They haven't got a clue. He even had me fooled, once. When we started here, Stuart Doyle was one of the kids who helped show us round. Telling us not to worry about getting lost, how it happens to everyone. Making us laugh over how he couldn't find the bogs on *his* first day and was so desperate he ended up in the girls' toilets. I thought that was so funny and that he was something special. I really did. You see it happening all the time – the new Year Sevens' hero-worship of him. Like he's a god bestowing gifts when he jokes with them. Or gives them tips about passing the ball they're kicking around at breaktimes.

It gives him a sort of power. Doyle is the only person I know who can help himself to the chocolate bar from some poor kid's lunchbox (the thing you've been saving till last and been looking forward to) and make you think he's doing you a favour – because he's chosen you. He does it with a smile and a pat on the head and, '*How's it going, then? Settling in are we?*' And wherever Doyle is, there's usually Sharples and Zimmer.

Not all kids are fooled by him though. Maybe they're not too happy to see their Snickers bar disappear, even if it's done with a smile and a joke. So, next time he's nice to everyone except the kid who complained. He might even decide to have a little joke with everyone about their big ears, or spots, or bad haircut. Sometimes he'll pick on a kid for no reason at all, except that it gets a big laugh. And everyone thinks he's this great funny guy. Except the kid they're laughing at.

'Right! I want this finished for homework. All books in my pigeonhole by tomorrow morning.'

I look up at Mr Day. I look down at my book. Somehow I've managed to write:

> 23rd November
> 1. Shylock, a Jew, agrees to lend some money to

Double English. Haven't been here for most of the time. My body has. Not the rest of me. Like astral projection. Lester was always going on about astral projection.

Feel sick. Amazing really that I didn't throw up over *The Merchant of Venice*.

'Edwin!' Mr Day beckons me over just as I reach the door. 'A moment of your time, please – *if* you can spare it!'

Edwin. Why does he always have to call me Edwin? Always gets a snigger. He used to call Lester *Miss Carroll* – that got a laugh. That's why I hate him. Lester had let his hair get quite long – kids had been winding him up. Think he picked up on that.

'Yes, Mr Day.'

'I don't know where you were this morning, but you certainly weren't here. I don't like people wasting my time. Everything's a laugh with you, isn't it Edwin? Well, you can take that smile off your face, because if you want to stay in my English set you'd better pull your socks up. I'm watching you. Go on – get out.'

I wasn't smiling. What have I got to smile about? It's my mouth – it's just the way it looks. See, it has these weird corners that turn up? So it looks like I'm smiling. Even when I'm dead depressed, like now. I can't help it can I? Lost count of the times I've had, *What are smirking about, Tully?* Or, *What's so funny, eh?* I blame my dad. It's his mouth too – which he got from Uncle Edwin. Maybe it's all Uncle Edwin's fault.

Someone taps me on the shoulder. 'Are you OK?'

'Uh – oh, yeah,' I say, with relief. Thought I might be turning round to find Doyle or one of his mates standing there, but it's that new girl, Caitlin, started last term. In my English group. She must have waited for me. She's at the bus stop each morning too. I saw her today, watching what they were doing to Lester. She's not like Sonya and her lot. She's got dark shiny hair, parted in the middle, pale skin . . .

'I just wanted to say . . .' She looks down at the bag she's clutching. 'I saw what happened. All of it. It was horrible what they were doing. And I think it was brave, really amazing what you did in the car park. I wanted to give a big cheer when you called out like that. But aren't you worried? I mean . . .'

I shrug and try to look like, *Me? Worried?* Then in the distance I see Sonya, Mel and Denise heading our way.

'Look, I've got to go – but thanks,' I say.

She spoke to me. She waited and spoke to me!

12.08 Dining hall

I find Carl and Ryan at the back. They're hunched over their trays at a table in the corner, like they're wary, on the lookout. They've got their heads down, talking.

'Here's the flaming mighty avenger,' Ryan mutters as I join them.

I sit down and search at the bottom of my bag for my mangled packed lunch. But I'm not hungry, so I start on the crisps – mainly for something to do with my hands. The jitters are getting to me.

They don't usually hang around school at lunchtimes, do they? I tell myself. Sixth Formers can go out. Can't help checking over my shoulder, though I had a good reccy before I came in. I see Ryan's eyes flicking around the hall.

'Relax, Ryan,' I say. 'They're not here. They'll be at the chippy or the café, won't they?'

'Them not being in the playground didn't stop them getting Dougie, did it?' he glares.

Carl's eating chips and making swirly patterns with his finger in a trail of salt on the table. 'From now on though we make sure we stay together,' he says.

'Oh great,' moans Ryan. 'We all hold hands and stay together every time one of us wants to take a pee, do we?'

Carl says, 'I'm not holding no one's hand. You can if you like. The main thing is we stick together, right?'

Ryan's eyes dart past me. He groans. 'Watch out.'

I turn my head and see Sonya and her mates approaching. What *now*? Just like to keep stirring it, don't they? Why aren't they with Brett, Clive and Jason as usual? Then I see the lads over the other side. Watching from the table by the window, smirking.

Sonya plonks her tray down on our table and sits next to me. 'Carry on – don't mind us.'

'Yeah, we don't want to miss anything,' Denise sniggers.

Carl leans back on his chair, hands behind his head. 'Can't leave us alone, can you?' he grins. 'Just can't get enough!'

It's not that he likes them. He just likes winding them up. The more he does it, the more they ask for it. I don't get it, I really don't.

'Where's Dougie, then?' Mel asks.

Does she know what happened to him?

'Why? You fancy him, then, do you Mel-an-ie?' Carl says, stretching out her name. We all know it's Carl that Mel fancies.

'Get off!' she snorts. 'He's pathetic!'

'She'd squash him flat,' splutters Denise.

Mel narrows her eyes into slits at Denise.

'That's not nice, that isn't, Denise,' Carl says. 'You ought to be nice to your friends.'

Why does he bother with them? *Do they know about Dougie?*

Sonya leans up close to me. 'Go on, Ed,' she whines. 'Tell us what Doyle was saying to you.'

'Everyone's saying it must be something really bad. Otherwise why the big secret, eh?' snorts Mel.

'Hey, should have seen your face!' Sonya sneers. 'You looked like you were pissing your pants!'

'Oh, yeah?' I force a smile to show what a cool customer I am. 'What about your pants then? You were practically throwing them at Stuart Doyle. Except he's not interested, is he?'

She doesn't like that. She glowers at me. Suddenly her jaw drops in horror.

'Oh my God!' she screams to Denise and Mel. 'You know what? Just realised something!' She wrinkles her nose at me. '*You* fancy Lester, don't you! Yeah, of course! Your secret boyfriend, isn't he? Yeah, that explains *everything*!'

'Eeeugh!' squeals Mel, rolling her eyes. 'That's disgusting!'

'Puke-making,' groans Denise. 'You're sick!'

Sonya's on her feet. 'Come on! Don't want to stay here. Not with a pervert!'

Ryan's frowning at me like he's believing it.

What have I done now? Stupid. Stupid. Stupid!

'Don't bother,' says Carl, standing up. 'We are leaving.' He leans over them and smiles, all calm like. 'Why so bitchy, eh? All that loud-mouthing and shrieking is real ugly. What makes you like that?'

'Yeah – all mouth,' adds Ryan.

'They think they're big women,' says Carl as he strides off.

There's a sudden guffaw of laughter and shrieks from the table where Sonya and Co have rejoined their mates. I keep my eyes aimed on the floor. Someone calls Carl's name. It's his girlfriend, Simone, beckoning to him from a table. 'Won't be a mo,' Carl says.

Ryan and me wait outside. 'Are you crazy!' starts Ryan. 'Every time you open your mouth you put your foot in it! They better not go round saying *I'm* gay! Flicking hell! All this crap – over Lester!'

Carl returns. We go in a threesome to the bogs. We have to wait for Ryan to have a fag. Puffs of smoke rise from the cubicles. You could get cancer in here. Carl fetches his football from his locker and we head for the pitch. I scan the playground as we cross and glance up at the windows. *Where are they? Doyle, Sharples and Zimmer?* Carl kicks the ball to Ryan. Paul and Gavin run over. Others join in. 'Five-a-side!' yells Carl.

13.04 Registration

'Douglas Wyman?' calls Mr Hargreaves for the second time. He looks at Carl.

'He had to go home. Got taken sick this morning,' says Carl.

I'm sweating from chasing the ball. My shirt sticks to my skin. But it's better than that sick sweat I felt this morning. For a few minutes I stopped thinking about Doyle, and everything. But I'm thinking about him now, aren't I? Think about something else. Think about the way you stole the ball away from Paul – that was nifty, that was. Passing it to Gavin. Carl's header.

Lester hates football. Running is more his thing. Maybe if he'd joined in a bit more he might've had an easier time. I mean – I'm not hyper about football, not like Carl and Ryan. But I go along with it, don't I? But he wouldn't. He was a bit bolshie like that. Yeah, maybe he did ask for it sometimes. When everyone else was kicking the ball around he'd go and sit with the girls, laughing and joking and calling out. And Carl would shout back, 'All right then, girls?' It was only a joke. Not like the stuff that happened later.

Sometimes Lester did ask for it. He let me down, remember? Maybe I *am* mad, getting done for Lester. I'm stupid. I'm not gay though. No way. Those girls are real bitchy. I hate them. I really hate them.

15.25 Art

The clay I'm trying to shape into a head is rubbish. I pretend that it's Stuart Doyle's head, and punch his nose in and give him two black eyes. Carl's working on his model of a footballer. He takes a pencil and uses the point to make two little nostrils in the nose. He's spent weeks on it. Used a cheese grater for all the little curly hair on the head, and a hairpin to carve all the folds in the ears. Ryan's working on a huge fist bursting up from the bottom of a giant mug.

'Dougie's gonna have some explaining to do about his trousers,' I say.

Carl shrugs. 'He'll think of something. His mum'd go bananas if he told her what really happened. She'd be down on the school like a ton of bricks. That would be really embarrassing.'

'Still can't believe what you did,' Ryan mutters. 'Why should Dougie suffer, just 'cos you couldn't keep your mouth shut?'

'Like Lester kept his mouth shut? Never helped him much, did it?'

'You think he's gonna thank you? It's only going to make it worse for him, isn't it? All you've done is get Dougie pissed on. He must be as mad as hell with you right now. And who's going to be next, eh?' He looks at Carl for back-up.

I say, 'Look, I've been thinking—'

'Makes a change,' Ryan snorts.

'Listen, maybe it was fluke – Dougie getting done like that. Maybe it was just some kids giving aggro. Maybe it was just coincidence that Doyle and the others happened to knock on the window at that moment.'

'Get real, willya?' Ryan glowers.

Carl leans forward. 'We've got to do some thinking about this – after school.'

'I can't.'

They look at me.

'Not till later. I can't help it.'

Carl sighs. 'OK – about seven? Round mine.'

I hear Mel's laugh from the other side of the room.

'I bet I know what they're laughing about.' Ryan glares at me. 'Well – I don't know about you, but I'm no poof.'

'Five minutes left!' Miss Clancy calls. 'All the clay back in the clay bins, please. Start clearing away. Leave anything ready for firing on the table by the sink.'

I roll up the mess of clay on my board and dump it in the bin. When I get back there's a small crowd round our table.

'Oh, look at his dinky little ears,' drools Leanne Tidman.

'He's blooming brilliant,' says Paul Young.

'Yeah, a right Leonardo da whatsit,' says Gavin Cox.

They're admiring Carl's football player.

■

Nothing else happened, nothing else happened, I tell myself as we join the streams of kids down the corridor. *Yeah, it was just a fluke, Dougie getting done like that. Just some kids giving some aggro.*

Someone gives me a shove. 'Poofter!'

Don't have to turn round to find out who it is. I'd know Brett Paine's voice anywhere. Suddenly I'm being jabbed behind the knees and I'm crashing to the floor. I see the backs of Brett, Jason and Clive disappearing. Kids pushing past.

'They try that on me and they've had it!' mutters Carl.

■

We catch up with Dougie and Ryan.

'Oi! Ryan!' It's Paul Young, waving from over by our lockers. 'There's a kid here looking for you!'

A small boy in football kit pushes his way through the crush. 'Ryan Rudge?'

'Yeah?'

The boy hands him a long white envelope and disappears.

Ryan looks at it. 'What . . . ?' *For the Attention of Ryan Rudge* is typed on it. He rips it open and takes out a letter.

It's a school letter. I can see the heading and the fancy school logo.

Ryan's face is a puzzle. 'This is old stuff! About a PTA

meeting or something.' He turns it over. 'What? What?' he squeals.

Typed on the back in big black print it says

YOU'RE NEXT

I groan.

Ryan frowns down at the print, his mouth hanging open. He looks at me, his face screwed up. 'What?' he says again. He turns it over, checking the envelope, as if searching for something that will tell him it's a mistake. 'Why me? Why me? What have I done? This is all your stupid fault! Bloody hell!'

I can't think of anything to say. We're getting pushed and shoved by kids scrambling round the lockers and pegs.

'We're gonna miss the bus,' I manage.

'Oh? Like I'm really worried about that! With Doyle and company menacing me from the back seat! Bloody hell!'

'If you want – come back with me,' says Carl.

They head off. Together.

The school bus

Tony Sharples's sitting at the back. He watches, smirking, as I make my way down the aisle. Sonya's sitting next to him. Keeping her eye on me, she whispers something in his ear. A horrible grin creeps over his face.

16.20 Home

'Where've you been, Ed? You're late!' My sister Ellie stands waiting at the front door. 'OK – Jack's waiting for you. I've left everything ready. Hope I haven't missed the bus. Gotta go! Seeya later!' The door slams behind her.

Jack looks up at me. I drop on to the sofa. 'What am I going to do, Jack?' I groan. 'What am I going to do?'

Jack crawls over to me and gives me the green rubber frog he's been chewing. It's covered with dribble.

'Thanks, Jack. I feel a lot better now.'

He snatches it back and shoves in it his mouth again. I pick him up and sit him on my knee.

'Listen, Jack. Some advice from your Uncle Ed. This is for when you can talk, right? Are you listening? No – leave my tie alone. I don't want slobber all over it again.'

He gazes up at me with his big blue eyes.

'Now, Jack – listen very, very carefully. Rule Number One: don't ever let your mouth take over from your brain, OK? And Rule Number Two: don't end up like Stuart Doyle. Got that? Good. 'Cos if you did, that would be really depressing. Rule Number Three: make the most of being a baby. This is the best and easiest part of your life, honest. Don't hurry walking and talking. That's right, shove your finger up your nose – enjoy it. When you get to my age you'll have to do that sort of thing in private.'

He bashes me on the nose with his frog. I put him

down on the floor and watch him play with his toes.

The day rewinds and replays in my head . . . The big question *What am I going to do?* keeps flashing up. What sickens me is the feeling of relief when I discovered that it was Ryan next and not me. Not that the feeling lasted long.

Something else keeps flashing up too. The look that Lester shot me after I called out to Stuart Doyle. I think I know what it meant now. It meant, *D'you know what you're letting yourself in for?* Suddenly I'm back to the Year Nine field trip. Lester – lying face down in a stream, his worksheets scattered, drenched. I watch him struggling to get up. Wading through the water, that empty look on his face as he tries to gather his pages together. Mrs Kepple coming over –

'What's going on here? Are you all right, Lester? What happened?'

'Just tripped.'

'Here –' A grinning Jason Stamp, handing him a sodden sheet, as if he had nothing to do with it. It had got to be that even the kids who were picked on were picking on Lester.

The clock is striking – three, four, five . . . it can't be. Where's Jack? 'Jack?'

I find him behind the sofa, a concentrated expression on his face. Know what that means. I give a sniff. Yep, right first time. 'Thanks Jack.'

I carry him into the bathroom, lay him on the baby

mat, take off his dungarees and peel off his disgusting nappy pad. 'How about swapping places, eh Jack?' I snatch a baby wipe and give his bum a polish. 'What I'd give to be six months old right now – not a care in the world. I wouldn't mind wearing nappies again, honest. No worries. No one out to get you –' I drop the mucky wipes down the loo and reach for a clean pad. 'You don't know what you've got coming Jack, you really don't.'

Wish I hadn't said that.

'Ignore that, Jack,' I tell him. 'Honest, everything's going to be great. Just learn from my mistakes, right?'

He chuckles, drops his frog and tries to grab my tie again. It keeps him busy while I fix the clean nappy.

I can't stop thinking about it all. I'm winding myself up. Think about something different. Talk – keep talking . . .

'Hey, how about that, Jack? A neat nappy or what? Admit it – I'm pretty good at all this baby stuff, aren't I? Yep, I am going to make some kid an excellent dad one day.'

I can't get over Jack – I really can't. This baby that came out of my sister. Can't get over his perfect tiny toes and fingers. The way he laughs. The way he makes *me* laugh. He creases me up, sometimes, he really does. Like the way he's a real person. He's amazing. And he's an excellent listener. I tell him stuff I'd never tell anyone else. Without him I'd be outnumbered by Mum and Ellie.

I couldn't take it in when Ellie told me she was pregnant. Just before Christmas last year it was. We were decorating the tree as a surprise for Mum when she got home from work. I thought Ellie was kidding. She's the last person you'd think would do something so dumb. Then she started crying, and I knew she wasn't.

'I haven't told anyone else except Dad.'

She'd told him when we'd been up to stay for the weekend. That explained a lot – the way Dad kept making a fuss, like how they had some sort of secret. She's always been a bit of a daddy's girl. And she'd been really quiet and moody on the train up. She didn't even have a serious boyfriend. It was some bloke she'd met at a club.

She'd been psyching herself up to tell Mum, and wanted me to be there when she did. She knew Mum would take it really badly. Don't get me wrong, Mum was quite understanding really. Upset too – yeah. But then she started taking over. Talking about seeing the doctor and getting it sorted. What Mum *couldn't* take was when Ellie told her she wasn't going to get rid it. That's all Jack was then. An IT. Ellie said she couldn't go through with that – it would feel like murder. She'd made up her mind. She'd have the baby and then it could be adopted. She wouldn't give in, no matter how much Mum tried to talk her into it. They were rowing all the time.

'I didn't plan this!' Ellie kept saying. 'I was careful –

really careful! It's not the baby's fault, is it?'

Ellie's the brainy one. Really brainy. Mum's boasting project she was. Mum had plans for Ellie. Getting pregnant at sixteen and having a baby during her GCSEs wasn't one of them.

That was a really bad Christmas.

Then when the baby was born, 'It' turned into Jack. And Ellie couldn't let him go.

'Who'd have thought a great little kid like you could have caused all those rows, eh?' I button up his dungarees. He chuckles like it's the funniest thing he's ever heard.

The way Mum fusses over Jack now, you'd never believe the way she went on before. And no way had I planned on becoming an uncle on my thirteenth birthday. One of the best presents I've ever had, if you want to know. Who'd have believed it? And I've got to hand it to Ellie. She's been amazing. Carried on going to school – big as a tank she was when she sat all her GCSEs. Jack was born four days later. And she got *eleven* A grades – all *starred* As. And now she's doing A levels part-time at City College. That's where she is now, seeing one of her tutors.

'OK, Jacko, time for din-dins.' I carry him into the kitchen, slip him into his highchair, make him a drink in his feeder cup and give it to him. 'There you go!'

I open the jar that Ellie's left on the worktop, pour the gunge into his Mr Wobble dish and heat it up.

'Here it comes!' He opens his mouth as I hold the spoon up and I shovel it in. And in those few seconds of not thinking, not talking, the rush of what I did hits me again.

'Listen, Jack, I've got to tell someone. I know you won't spread it around.'

He opens his mouth again and I shove in another spoonful.

'I did something really stupid today, Jack. And I'm scared. No kidding. Really, really scared. It was like this, see—'

His hands splat the food in the dish. 'Aw! Jack!' Orange gunge all over my shirt! He laughs. I grab the dishcloth.

The phone starts ringing.

'Hello?'

I hear slow heavy breathing in my ear.

'Who is this?'

The breathing gets louder.

I slam the phone down and then dial one four seven one. A firm female voice says, 'You were called today at seventeen thirty-two hours. The caller withheld their number.'

I replace the receiver. It rings instantly. More breathing – then it changes into a choking groan, like someone being strangled. I cut it off – stand like an idiot holding the receiver.

The front door bangs.

Jack's massaging cheesy pasta bake into his hair now.

Mum's voice calls from the hall, 'Hi! I'm home!'

I shove the phone back on the wall. It rings again. I snatch it up.

'Mrs Tully?' says a voice.

'Hold on – she's just got in,' I say, relieved.

The voice changes to a croak. 'We know. Just want to let you know we are watching. All the time. We are everywhere.' Sniggering in the background – then a click as the line goes dead.

I dash to the window and peer up the road. Too dark to see properly.

Mum comes into the kitchen with a bag of shopping. 'And how's my clever little Jack . . . Ed – for heaven's sakes! Look at him! Did you have to let him get into such a mess?' She grabs the cloth from me. 'Who was that on the phone?'

'Double-glazing or something.'

'How was school, then?' she asks, like she does every day.

'OK.'

'You'd better take that shirt off and put it to soak! Honestly, Ed – what a mess to come home to!'

■

'Mum – can you give me a lift over to Carl's?'

'What about your homework?'

'It's about homework.'

'And what's wrong with your bike?'

'Nothing. It's just that Carl's asked to borrow my amplifier and I can't manage that on my bike.'

'A complete waste of money, that was. Months of driving us up the wall with that guitar and now you hardly look at it.'

'Please, Mum. You could give Ellie a driving lesson at the same time.'

'Yeah, good idea,' says Ellie. 'Have to go now, though, before I get Jack ready for bed.'

19.10 Carl's house

'You're late,' says Carl.

'Yeah. Sorry.'

He frowns at my amplifier on his doorstep. 'What you brought that for?'

'You're borrowing it, right?'

'We're down in the basement – in the den,' he says.

Carl's mum comes into the hall. 'Hello, Eddie,' she smiles. 'How's you?'

'Great, thanks.'

I follow Carl down the steps. Carl's dad has fitted the basement out with an exercise bike and weights and a workbench. There's a battered old sofa and garden recliner too, which makes it really cramped. A big NO SMOKING sign is tacked to the door. Ryan's pedalling away on the bike. Dougie's fully stretched out on the recliner, plugged into his mini CD-player. He ignores me and carries on nodding to the beat. No one says anything. It feels like I've interrupted a secret meeting.

'Five point six kilometres,' Ryan announces, staring down at the gauge.

I put the amp down and flop on to the sofa. Carl perches on the workbench and stares down at the amp. 'Are you going to tell me why I'm borrowing this, then?'

'I needed a lift. It was the only excuse I could think of at the time.' I tell him about the phone calls. 'I thought it might be a bit risky coming over on my bike, just in case they were – you know – following me.'

'Huh!' says Ryan to Dougie. 'Now he knows what it feels like.'

But Dougie's not listening and his eyes are closed. The base thumps out from his CD-player.

'Who d'you think it was, then?' asks Carl.

'I dunno. The voice on the last call was definitely male.'

Dougie takes off his headphones and stares at my amp. 'What you brought that amp for?'

I go over it all again and tell him about the phone calls. He shrugs as if to say, *Don't look to me for sympathy*.

'It could've been Doyle or one of his mates,' Ryan sneers. 'Anyone, come to that. I mean, Doyle wasn't the one who peed on your trousers, was he, Dougie? He's getting other people doing stuff for him.'

'They'd have been using a mobile,' Dougie says to

the amp. 'If they were outside your house, watching.'

At least Dougie's talking to me. Sort of. 'Look, Dougie – Ryan, I feel really bad—'

'Bit late, isn't it?' Ryan snaps.

'Who do we know that's got mobiles, then?' he asks, after a bit.

'Dougie, for starters,' says Carl. 'Thousands. Sonya's went off in English. Brett, Jemma, Doyle . . .' He strings a list of names. 'Half the kids in school probably.'

'Not half,' Ryan says, as if this going to help.

'Did you *see* anyone outside your house?' Dougie asks sulkily.

'Nope.'

Ryan climbs off the exercise bike and flops on to the sofa next to me and folds his arms. 'How come they knew his mum had just got home, then?'

'He told them, didn't he, dummy?' Dougie sighs wearily. 'The voice said, "*Mrs Tully?*" And Ed told them to hold on – she'd just got in. Then they said, "*we know.*" They weren't outside watching. Just winding him up.'

I feel stupid.

'You're getting off easy, you are,' Ryan grunts without looking at me.

'Look Ryan, you think I planned this? You think I like what's happening?'

'Yeah – but it was *you* who had to open his big

mouth. Why should *we* get it, eh?' His voice goes into a squeal.

'Fifty-nine quid those trainers cost!' says Dougie. 'I worked my butt off saving up for those. Had to tell my mum I'd been sick. I had to clean everything up! It was disgusting, that's what it was!'

'Yeah, I know. I'm sorry! I really am. What else can I say? But can't you see? That's how Doyle's getting back at me. By getting at you!'

'Is that s'posed to make us feel better?' Ryan squeaks. 'I still don't get it! I mean – Lester cops it all the time from Brett and his lot. It's been going on for ages. You ignore all that! But when Doyle has a go, you decide to make a joke of him! Him of all people. In front of everyone!'

Ryan looks really scared. But not as scared as I feel.

'I dunno. Just pisses me off the way he enjoys humiliating people. I didn't stop to think, did I? I dunno.' I shrug.

'Maybe Sonya was right,' Ryan says to Dougie and Carl. He looks at me. 'Maybe you *do* fancy Lester. Miss him, do you?'

Carl scratches his head. Dougie glances at me, then stares down at his feet.

'I mean,' Ryan goes on, 'you two used to go round together all the time, right? Practically glued together – till you joined The Diehards. Always thought you was weird.'

I hate the sneery look on his face.

'Yeah, OK. I fancy Lester.' I can't believe I just said that.

'What?' bleats Ryan.

All three of them are staring at me like their eyes are going to pop out. Dougie blinks at me, then at Carl. Ryan's face is going through contortions. Carl shakes his head.

'Hold on, hold on,' he says. 'Are you telling us that you *are* gay?'

It's almost funny. It's scary too.

'No! I'm ruddy not! And no way do I fancy Lester! I'm just getting sick of Ryan going on about it!'

Dougie says, 'Ha, ha. Very clever. He really got you going there, Ryan.'

'What's he playing at?' Ryan glowers. 'Aren't we supposed to be deciding what we're gonna do about this trouble you've landed us in? I'm only saying what people are thinking. Loads of kids thought you two were weird. Why say you're gay if you're not, eh?' He looks at the others, like he wants backing up.

'It's you that keeps going on about it!' I tell him. 'What's *your* problem, Ryan?'

Dougie sighs heavily. 'This is wasting time.'

'Tell that to Ryan,' I say. 'He's the one who keeps on and on about Lester. Anyway, how come everyone's so sure *Lester* is gay? Eh? Brett started that. You believe what Brett says, do you?'

'OK but Lester acts like a girl, doesn't he?' says Ryan. '*You* stopped going around with him, remember? Don't have a go at me!'

I'm thinking, *No, actually. He doesn't act like a girl. People like you, Ryan, say he does.*

I say, 'I didn't stop going round with him. *He* stopped going round with me, remember?'

'Yeah. After The Wall of Death,' nods Dougie. 'That was weird. You've got to admit, he's weird.'

Carl stands up. 'This is getting us exactly nowhere.'

'Too right,' agrees Ryan. He waves the letter. 'All I know is I got this and *he's* still talking about *poor old Lester*.' He puts on a stupid girly voice.

'Well, maybe now you've got some idea of what he's been getting day after day,' I mutter.

'Me? Why does he keep having a go at me?' Ryan asks.

'Leave it!' says Carl. He leans against the wall and folds his arms. 'This is the way I see it. What's happened, has happened. We're all in this, whether we like it or not.'

'And I don't,' Ryan mutters.

Carl ignores him. He looks at me. 'That was a dumb, stupid thing to do, Ed. Even though I agree that Doyle and his mates are a load of tossers. But you've put us all in it.'

'You can say that again,' nods Ryan. 'You wanna know what I think? Ed got us into this, so he can get us out of it. I think Ed ought to apologise – grovel even. It's all about face, isn't it? You can't go round making Doyle look stupid and get away with it. Doyle had to do something, didn't he? Maybe if Ed did a bit a grovelling – suck up, apologise, anything – well he might let him off the hook, eh? And us with him. Why should we get all this grief just because Ed decides to mouth off? Personally, I think Lester had it coming.'

He looks round at Dougie. Dougie looks at Carl. Carl looks at me.

'Well?' he says.

I see myself grovelling. I see Doyle and his mates laughing their heads off – and worse stuff. Would he let me off? Would he? It'd be worth it – wouldn't it? Then I see Lester standing there being humiliated. And Doyle's smug smile.

'No,' I say.

'We're all in this! It's not up to you!' Ryan snaps. 'We all have a say in this.' He turns to Dougie. 'Come on, Dougie!'

Dougie leans forwards on his arms and stares down at the carpet. 'It wouldn't work,' he announces without looking up. 'Doyle's enjoying this. It's a game to him. He'd love to make Ed grovel. But then he'd just carry on anyway. He wants to teach him a lesson – not forgive him. He's not flipping Jesus, is he?'

Carl nods. 'Ed's right about Doyle using us to get at

him. All this arguing – it's just what he wants, isn't it? If he could see us now, he'd be well pleased. It's him and the others we ought to be getting mad at. And that's what I really hate – the way he's using all of us. You want to be used by Doyle, do you?' He looks hard at Ryan. 'Well, me – I do not like being used. Who do they think they are, eh?'

'That's easy to say,' says Dougie. 'You don't get no choice! I didn't ask to be pissed on, did I?'

'I know that – and I bet they try and have a go at me too. What I'm saying is: get mad at Doyle – not at each other, right? Because that's just what he wants – and we're playing right into his hands. Do you really wanna do that? Don't you see? He's winning already. Unless we stick together, we are in trouble. So no more sniping at each other, right?'

He looks at Ryan. Ryan shrugs then sighs.

He looks at me. I nod.

Dougie says, 'At least now we know what his tactics are, don't we?'

'We're agreed then,' says Carl. 'Because there is no way I'm going to let Doyle – or anyone else – walk all over me.'

Ryan looks up. 'So what *are* we supposed to do?'

'First, we don't let them see what they want to see.'

'What's that?' asks Ryan.

'That they're getting to us. We act like nothing's happened.'

'And we don't take any chances,' says Dougie. 'We don't go anywhere on our own. We watch each other's backs all the time.'

'Starting with mine,' says Ryan. 'Seeing as I'm next on the list!'

'My mum's coming to pick me up at nine – we can drop you off at home if you like,' I offer.

Ryan sighs and takes a packet of cigarettes from his jacket. Carl shakes his head slowly.

'Aw, go on! I need it. Who's gonna know?'

'My dad,' says Carl. 'He's got the nostrils of a bloodhound.'

Ryan slides down into the seat. 'I might bunk off tomorrow,' he mutters. 'They can't get me if I'm not there. We could all bunk off.'

'Oh yeah? All week?' says Dougie. 'Don't you think the school might notice? The office rings your parents on the second day. They even rang my mum today – at work, would you believe – because I'd walked out without telling anyone. It's all part of their new anti-skiving off campaign.'

'If we stick together, we should be OK,' says Carl. 'It's only till Friday, innit?'

'I bloody well hope so,' mutters Ryan.

Carl looks at me and shakes his head. 'Hey – I'll never forget the look on Doyle's face when you held up your fingers like that and called out. And when everyone laughed. Man –' he grins '– that was really something. I am never gonna forget that.'

Then Ryan says, 'No – and Doyle's never gonna forget it either.'

∎

What's the time? One thirty-nine a.m. Don't want to close my eyes. Keep seeing these horrible scenes. I'm in all of them. Is this what it's like for Lester? Lying awake, wondering what's going to happen to you the next day. Is he lying awake, like me?

Hey! Lester! Can you hear me?

Is he gay? I mean – just 'cos people say it . . .

What if *I'm* gay! How can you tell? Can you be gay and not know it? I mean, I miss him, I really miss him, sometimes. And I'm thinking about him, aren't I? Does that mean I'm gay? Does it?

What about that time he borrowed his mum's clothes? . . . No – that was just a joke. He never *behaved* like a girl – no way! But then you hear of blokes who are commandos and stuff who are gay.

Never had a proper girlfriend though, have I? Not really. Had a laugh with them, that's all. But I *fancy* them – I fancy them all the time, don't I? Just that they don't fancy me. *Must* be normal if I fancy them. Hey, maybe Caitlin fancies me! She waited for me – said I was brave! She's got a really nice face – that pale skin and blue eyes. Oh help –

it's changing into Doyle's face—

    Sit up. Need a drink . . .

■

The face staring back at me from the bathroom mirror looks like a ghost. *Astral projection.* The words pop into my head. Lester was always on about astral projection. He'd found a book about it in the library. Mad about supernatural stuff he was. The one-three-threes he called them – the library code for the spooky-weird section. Ghosts, poltergeists, alien abductions – he was really hooked on that sort of stuff.

I'd go round to his house and it'd be, 'Hey – you won't believe this. It's amazing. Just listen.' And he'd read bits out – totally freaky stories. And he'd trawl the internet too. You wouldn't believe the seriously strange stuff that's out there.

Astral projection is about how some people think it's possible to separate your spirit from your body. Sometimes it just happens. Like how some people who've been under anaesthetic say they suddenly found themselves floating above the operating table. They could look down and see themselves lying there. They could see the surgeon and the nurses, and watch themselves being sliced open – hearing every word. Then suddenly they'd be zoomed back inside their body again. And afterwards, they could remember it all and report everything they'd seen and heard exactly as it had happened.

What these books were saying was you could *learn* to do it. People have been studying it for thousands of years – the Egyptians, the Tibetans, the Greeks. It takes loads of practice. But eventually you learn to make the spirit part of you – your consciousness – separate from your physical body. Then you'd be able to float up, look down and see your body lying or sitting wherever you left it. With practice you could train yourself to travel wherever you wanted to go. You'd start with easy stuff, like going into the next room. Then there are different levels to progress to. You could travel at amazing speeds. Pass through walls and objects. Fly above seas and mountains. Soar over volcanos. According to Lester, some masters of astral projection could travel across time barriers and visit previous lives – that takes years and years of meditation and training. He started practising.

What really got to me was this story he told me, about a holy man who after years of study and meditation had become a true master of astral projection. Then he was arrested – for sheltering political prisoners or something. He was thrown into prison. They put him under the most terrible tortures. His torturers could never understand how he survived the pain. Why he never even called out or screamed. They didn't know about astral projection – that he wasn't really there. His body was. But his spirit was miles away. Sitting on top of a beautiful mountain, watching the sun rise. Eventually, he was released. His body was broken, but he recovered. They hadn't been able to break his spirit. Later, one of the torturers became a follower . . . Yeah – there were loads of stories like that.

Then one evening I got this phone call. It was Lester, yelling, 'I did it! I did it!' He told me he'd been lying on his bed when it'd happened. 'I was floating up to the ceiling! Honest! And I could see this gap behind the picture rail – there was this spider there.' But then, he said, he got too excited and suddenly zoomed back to his body. 'I did it! I really did it!' he kept saying. He told me he'd climbed up later to check, and sure enough there was the spider behind the rail. That was the first time.

The second time he claimed he'd actually managed to astrally project himself from his bedroom into the kitchen. Only for a split second. But just long enough to see his mum making his sandwiches. He'd been disappointed because she was doing tuna again and he'd asked for cheese and tomato. Instantly – zoom! He was back on his bed. The scary part was that I sort of believed him.

He kept nagging me to try – but no way. What if I couldn't get back? And after that, well there was The Wall of Death. And we broke up, didn't we?

'*What made you do that?*' That's what Carl asked. Why did I flip like that in the car park?

Want to know why? I'd been kidding myself that no one could hurt Lester. He wasn't there. His body was – but not his spirit. Because Lester had mastered the art of astral projection. Yeah, I know – sounds pathetic. I kept telling myself the real Lester was flying over oceans. Riding an iceberg. He always looked so still. Impassive. Like he truly wasn't there. *Astral projection*, I'd kid myself. *Good on ya, Lester. They can't reach you.*

It was that drip on his nose. That was the reason I flipped. Lester was there all right. It wasn't just his body standing there. It was the real Lester. He'd always been there. Being slowly, painfully tortured. I'd known that all the time. I don't believe any of that stuff. I'd been lying to myself, hadn't I? Because I'm a coward.

It destroyed me, that drip. It really did. How can I explain that to anyone?

TUESDAY

The Wall of Death

I'm caught in the barbed wire at the top. I look down.
A tiny little figure looks up at me. The wire's wrapped
round my leg. I'm struggling to get free – slivers of
skin peel back. I can see this thick vein, transparent
like a plastic tube, pumping blood up my leg. Keep
still! Don't move! If you cut the vein, you're dead. Hey,
look! My other leg. It's in shreds. Blood's spurting
everywhere like a fountain. I watch with interest,
calmly . . .

Aaaaaaaaagh! I'm falling! Help! I'm falling!

What's happening now? I'm slowing down. It's higher
than I thought, The Wall of Death. It must be miles
high! Hey – falling is nothing at all. It's amazing! Like
flying. What was I worried about? It's a synch. This is
OK, this is. I'm drifting now, hovering. What's that down
there? It's a body – a boy – sprawled on the ground
below. It's me! I must be dead, then. Is this what dead
feels like? It's OK. It's nice.

There's Lester! Standing over my body, looking down
at it. I hover over him. 'That's your fault, Lester,' I'm
calling. He can't hear me.

'Quitters United,' he says to himself. 'Quitters United'.

■

Uh? Uh? What's going on? It's dark. Sit up. What's the time? Put on the light. Did I really scream – or did I dream that? Where's my watch? Five thirty-seven! Aw – gonna be so knackered at school. Oh God – school. Don't think about school. That was so real – so real. Look at me. I'm covered in sweat. That was some weird dream.

The Wall of Death. I can see it like I'm standing in front of it. It wasn't a wall at all. That was just The Diehards' name for it. It was a wire fence really. Three, maybe four metres high. Seemed like miles. There were KEEP OUT signs all over the place. Behind the fence was the old railway station's goods yard – full of old lock-ups and boarded-up workshops. All gone now – it's a Tesco's superstore.

The Wall of Death was to stop you breaking in. Just inside was this electricity substation. There was a big warning sign on it: DANGER OF DEATH! That's how the fence got its name. In case you couldn't read, there was a black silhouette picture of a man thrown off his feet, like he was being electrocuted – a big zig-zag of electricity shooting into his chest – like that bit in the film, *The Omen*, where the priest is skewered by shards of glass.

Along the top of the fence were these rows of barbed wire. You'd have to be a moron to try and climb over it. I know, because I nearly killed myself trying.

The Diehards. What a dumb name. When I was twelve, though, I thought it sounded dead cool. They always seemed to be having a laugh – rigging up that rope-swing over the river, mucking about in their den down the spinney. I was a bit wary of them – but jealous too. There were four of them: Matt, a square, tough, short kid – he moved away. Totally mad. They used to call him Mad Matt. Always doing crazy things. Walked across the girders on Hoopers Bridge once – a least a fifteen metre drop to the river. Then there was Ryan, Carl and Dougie. Yeah – Watch-out-don't-scuff-my-new-trainers-Dougie! But he wasn't such a fussy dresser then. He only hung around with them because of Carl.

I was dying to have a go on that swing. Every time Lester and I saw them together, they seemed to be having a great time. It was the end of the summer holidays – our first year at high school. I thought maybe we could join in with them, only for a bit. Lester wasn't keen. He said things wouldn't be the same – we were better on our own. He thought The Diehards were sad.

But things *weren't* the same. Something was different. Lester had got to be real moody sometimes. I never knew why. We'd been friends since we were five. I couldn't understand what was going on. It was getting boring and I was feeling a bit pissed off with him. That day he was supposed to call for me. All morning I waited. It'd happened quite a few times. In the end I pedalled over to his. He said he'd forgotten. Probably too busy astrally projecting himself.

For something to do, we bike down to the river. And there they are – The Diehards – on their rope-swing. I'm so fed up I shout to ask if we can have a go. They get into a little huddle.

'What did you go and do that for?' moans Lester. 'I don't want to hang around with them.'

Matt beckons us over. Lester's dawdling, acting like he's not interested.

Matt says, 'Yeah. OK. But you've got to pass the initiation test first.' They start laughing as if they know something we don't.

So I say, 'What's that then?'

Matt gives a nod and all four of them chant together, '*All Diehards must climb The Wall of Death.*'

Sounds pathetic now, but then, it sounded dead impressive. And really scary. We didn't have a clue what they were on about. Then, Matt starts explaining. And the more I hear about it the more I'm going off the idea. So I'm acting like I'm not that bothered about their stupid rope-swing. No way am I going to climb The Wall of Death. It's not just climbing. You have to get over the barbed wire at the top, down the other side, touch the electricity box, then back over again. Lester's looking at me, like he's saying, *Didn't I tell you this was a stupid idea?*

'Are you up for it, then?' Matt says. His pushes his face into mine and grins, 'Or are you scared, eh?'

I tell him I've got better things to do than climb stupid fences.

Matt turns on Lester. 'You can get lost!' he sneers. 'We don't want no queers, OK? No girly-wirlies!'

I see Lester's white face glow pink. Someone wolf-whistles and they start laughing and Ryan does this jokey poncey walk.

It was that first year at high school that Lester began getting stick. But I think that was when it really hit me what was going on. I remember the sick feeling in my stomach.

I pick up my bike, wishing I hadn't bothered, thinking Lester was right all along. I just want to get away. I'm feeling stupid. Angry too. Mixed-up angry. Angry with Matt and the others. With myself for getting involved. And with Lester. I mean, why couldn't he just make more of an effort to fit in? Like on this particular day he's wearing this embarrassing waistcoat that he'd found in some charity shop. Sometimes it was like he was doing it on purpose. I'm thinking, *What if he is gay? They'll think I am too. What if I am? And if I leave with him now, they'll really believe it!* – though I was pretty clueless about what it all meant.

I get on my bike.

They start chanting, 'Scared! Scared! Scared!'

Lester still hasn't moved. 'I'm not scared,' he says. 'I'll do it. No problemo.'

He was always saying that. '*No problemo!*'

I can't believe what I'm hearing. Now I'm having a major panic attack. I mean, Lester knows how terrified I am about heights. I throw him a look, but he just shrugs.

'OK,' grins Matt. 'But if you get killed, don't blame me.'

And they set off for this wall. So I have to trail along, piss-scared but trying to look hard and desperately trying to think of some way out. There was no way out. If Lester did it and I didn't – well I'd be on my own wouldn't I?

Why did Lester do that to me? He *made* me do it. *He* made me climb that wall. I had no choice. I was really mad with him for putting me through that. I thought I was going to die. No kidding.

When we get there, Matt says, 'Ryan will show you how easy it is, won't you Ryan?'

That's what amazes me about Ryan. Gets wound up over really stupid things – like he can never take joke, or when people have a go. But when it comes to risking garroting himself on barbed wire and being torn to pieces, it's like he can't wait to do it.

So we watch Ryan scramble up. How's he going to get over that barbed wire? It's impossible. I can hardly bear to look – I'm feeling ill. Suddenly, Ryan's swinging himself over – like a somersault. How did he do that? I'm thinking, *I'm never gonna be able to do that*! I was having a heart attack just watching. He scrambles down the other side, dashes to the box – back again, clawing his way up.

Watch, I tell myself. *Watch how he does it*. But he's so quick. It's like a handstand on wire – like he's flying. His legs making a perfect arc against the sky as he swings over. Then he's scrambling down and suddenly he's standing on the ground doing a victory dance.

The others clap him on the back and they link arms, swaying from side to side, singing, '*Die-hards! Die-hards! Die-hards, Die-hards!*' Singing it to the tune of *Amazing Grace*. That was so impressive, that singing and shouting. Part of me wanted to be swaying along with them – but the other part just wanted out.

'See? Dead easy!' Ryan grins.

'We've all done it. Loads of times,' says Matt. 'Oi, Carl – show him your scars.'

Carl pulls up the leg of his jeans. There's a jagged scar on his shin. I can see the little holes where the stitches must have gone. I whistle to show how impressed I am.

'Your turn now,' nods Matt. 'Who's gonna go first?'

Lester walks up to the fence. He stares up at it. Then he starts to climb, taking his time, calmly testing handholds and footholds in the loops. He stops when he reaches the barbed wire, like he's having second thoughts – but he's just working out how to get over.

They start jeering and hooting.

Don't do it! I'm urging inside my head. *Don't do it! Come down, you idiot – then I won't have to do it either! Please! Come down! I just want to get out of here!*

They start chanting, 'Scared! Scared! Scared! Scared! Scared!'

He moves up, his feet are just below the lines of barbed wire now. He straightens up, teetering like a tightrope walker. Arms up, swaying against the sky, like he's sun-worshipping or something. I'm feeling sick. It goes quiet. All of us staring up. *He's stuck*, I think. I can't see how he can get over. I can't look any more.

'Get on with it, willya!' Matt bellows.

Now Lester's got a leg over – no! He's slipped! He's dangling – spinning in mid-air. It's his waistcoat – it's caught on the wire. He's kicking with his feet, trying to reach the fence. He bounces against it, makes a grab and pulls himself on to it.

I'm sweating like a pig. I know I'm never gonna be able to climb that fence.

Lester's clambering down now – he runs to the box. Scrambling up again. At the top he takes his time. Manages to lean over and get a hold on the fence – then does a sort of rolling dive. The rest looks easy. He lands neatly.

'No problemo,' he shrugs, folding his arms. They're

scratched to bits. There's blood on his trousers. His white face glistens with sweat.

'Your turn,' says Matt to me.

■

I still don't know how I did it. I just sort of blanked out. My hands were sweating so much I had to keep wiping them on my jeans. The first bit was OK – but I made the mistake of looking down. Then I just froze. So I closed my eyes and felt my way up.

There was this little voice in my head saying, *It would be easier to let go. Go on – let go – fall! Just get it over with! You don't have to do it. Better to break a few bones than be ripped to bloody shreds. Doesn't matter if you end up in hospital. There'll be trouble then – and serve them right.*

I hated them for putting me through it. I hated Lester too. Why was he doing this to me? It seemed like I was climbing for ever. Suddenly I was at the top. I remember squinting up. The wire was silhouetted against the sky – a bright blue sky – these wispy clouds skudding along. Made me dizzy – as if it was me that was moving, not the sky. The barbs were glinting like little daggers. It felt unreal, like I was in some virtual reality game. Panicking – couldn't see where I could get a hold – not without ripping my hands to pieces. I knew if I looked down I'd had it.

I was wearing my old parka. I managed to get it off and threw it over the wire. Tried straddling over at first, but kept getting visions of wires up my bum. I could hear them laughing and jeering below. Then got stuck – I thought I was going to be stuck there for ever. So in total panic I just sort of dived. Somehow managed to grab on to the fence on the other side. It was such a relief to have survived that climbing down seemed easy after that. I touched the box and started back up again.

Then something weird happened. The adrenaline must have been pumping like mad and as I climbed back up, I felt this enormous rush! I can hardly remember how I got back over the wire. I knew I was getting cut, but I didn't feel a thing. Suddenly I'm standing where I started – on the other side of the fence. I was on this huge high – like I was on drugs or something, like I could do anything! I was leaping up and down – the most amazing feeling I've ever had. I thought, *I know why Matt does these mad things! I know why now!*

They start to sing. '*We are the champions! We are the champions!*' And I'm singing too – arm in arm, swaying – and singing at the tops of our voices, feeling like I'd never been so alive before. Swaying and singing – all except Lester. He's wandered over to his bike and stands there, waiting for me.

I see the blood then – seeping through my tee-shirt. My jeans are torn to pieces. There's little tears in my legs and hands and on my chest. And I think, *Wow! War wounds.* I can't even feel them.

Then having survived all that – having been torn to bloody shreds by barbed wire and risked falling the height of Everest to certain death on the concrete below – I see Lester pedalling off. He doesn't say anything. Not a word. It's like he's mad at me or something.

And that was our last time together as mates. How could he do that? He never phoned, called round or anything. Why did he do that?

On my way home I threw up.

Strange summer, that was. The summer when everything changed.

08.09 *The bus stop*

Slow down, slow down. No sign of the bus yet. Hang about till you see it coming. Don't want to get there too soon. No sign of Lester either – ahead or behind. No big surprise. Bunked off I expect. Thought about it myself – just for a day, or a week. Faking sick or something. I even tried out impersonating Mum's special telephone voice: *I'm phoning to say that my son Ed Tully will not be attending school as he wants to make the most of the remaining few days of his tragically short life.*

I could still skive off, couldn't I? Could I? After what happened to Dougie and Ryan? They'd really love me then – I *don't* think.

How did Lester keep going? Getting that crap every

day. The teachers could see it. Don't tell me they didn't. But Lester's like that.

'Oi! Winnie! Winnie the Pooh!'

Oh yeah, thanks Mel. I'm at the bus stop already. Act like I don't hear. Not digging up that stupid old game, are they? Really back in the infants now. I used to hate my name – didn't mind the Winnie part so much. It was when they shortened it to Pooh. When you're a little kid that gets to you, it really does. '*Look out! Here comes Pooh!*' And they're running round, holding their noses, going. '*POOH! POOH!*' Used to get quite upset about it.

'Where's your boyfriend today then, *Pooh*?' says Denise.

Where's the ruddy bus? That's what I want to know. It's crawling along. It's got to be at least ten minutes late now. Still no Lester. Maybe he's had enough. Hey – maybe he's told his mum. Maybe she's been up the school. It'll all come out. Sonya, Brett and his mates – the whole lot will get called to the Head's office. Doyle and Sharples, too – God, I'd love to see that. And Friday will just be – an ordinary beautiful Friday.

No Doyle or Sharples yet. Funny. Sonya and her friends look a bit lost without someone to show off to.

The bus pulls up. About time.

Uh? What's going on? Why's Ryan sitting next to Andrew Paisley? Thanks for the loyalty, mate! Doing eye-signals over his shoulder. What's he trying to tell me? Ah – now I see. Sharples and Zimmer. They're sitting in *our* seat. They're staring at me – blank faces – like I'm some sort of experiment.

'Move will ya! Spazzer!'

I get shoved from behind. I turn to see Mel.

'Ugh!' She reels back. 'Aw – Winnie! Your breath! Halitosis or what! Your breath is poison! You ought to get that seen to. Watch out everyone! It's a killer!'

Hoots and laughs.

Sonya's voice. 'That's why he's called Pooh!'

'Pooh! Pooh! Pooh! Pooh!' All three of them. Shrieking and laughing.

I crash into the nearest empty seat. Caitlin's making her way down. She doesn't look at me but gives a tiny, secret thumbs-up signal as she passes. Can't see Doyle anywhere.

'That's our seat.'

The freckled faces of the ginger twins look down at me. I shrug and look out of the window.

08.42 School

'They got me! This morning! They got me!'

Ryan muttering under his breath, as soon as I catch him up. Dougie and Carl are with him.

'How?'

'What'd they do?' says Carl.

Ryan shakes his head. 'Never want to go through that again. Not ever.'

He's glaring at me. He's really jittery. It must be something really bad.

'What happened?' But I'm not sure I want to know.

'Flicking hell! Why should you ruddy care?' he spits. 'You've got a bloody nerve!'

'Just tell us what happened, Ryan,' says Carl, calmly.

'Right, I'm going along the road, see – and I turn the corner and there they are, waiting for me. I'm thinking, this is it – they're going to do me. Then Zimmer starts shoving me back down the alley. You know, that alley behind the garages? And Sharples pushes me up against the door. He's got his hands round my neck, like this see?'

He demonstrates. His neck has pale bruise marks and scratches.

'I tell you – I've never been so scared in all my life.'

'What'd they do?' asks Dougie.

'Isn't that enough?' says Ryan. 'You try having your air supply cut off. He was strangling me. I couldn't breathe!' He rubs his neck again. 'Anyway, it's not what they did. It's what they said.' Ryan turns to look at me. 'You're not gonna like this.'

'Ryan! Just tell me!'

'OK. Dougie was wrong. There's going to be a fight. For definite.'

'Get away,' Carl says. 'Doyle was winding you up. He's never gonna do anything that'd land him in trouble with school. I can't see Doyle in a stupid scrap. No way!'

'Doyle wasn't there, was he?' snaps Ryan. 'Just Sharples and Zimmer. And I'm telling you – there's gonna be a fight.'

'Look Ryan,' I ask. 'Just tell us exactly – word for word – what they said, will you?' Ryan always has his own version of stuff.

He gives a little laugh, like he's pleased to be delivering bad news.

'Right. They've got me up against the wall, see. Then Zimmer says in my ear, "*You are the chosen one.*" '

'What?' we all say.

'*You are the chosen one,*' he repeats. 'That's what he said. "*You are the messenger.*" Then Sharples says, "*Tell that little shite,*" that's you,' Ryan nods at me. ' "*Tell that little shite the challenge is accepted. The time and place have been decided. He will be informed in –*" Hold on, hold on,' Ryan frowns – ' "*In due course.*" That's it. Then he says, "*He must prepare for battle.*" Then Zimmer says "*And to be knocked senseless.*" His breath stank of garlic. Oh yeah, and, on your own. "*He must come alone,*" that's what he said – if you want to be exact. That's it.' He shrugs. 'Except all the time they're killing themselves, like they think it's so funny. Then they walk off. And I have to walk behind them to the bus stop trying not to get too close. And then I have to wait for the bus with them staring at me.' He shrugs again. 'Well, I don't know about you, but that sounds to me like there's going to be a fight – *you* are going to get done.' He looks really jittery.

'Is that it?' says Carl. 'They didn't rough you up any?'

'What's the matter?' Ryan squeaks. 'Isn't that enough?' He rubs his neck.

Then Dougie says quietly, 'But it doesn't mean it's gonna be Doyle personally, does it? Remember, I'm speaking from experience here. He gets other people to do his dirty work. If someone's gonna beat you up, it won't be Doyle. And you won't know who – that's clever that is. Man! What a mess.'

'How comes Ryan gets off so lightly?' Dougie mutters as we walk in. 'And how come I get pissed on? There's no justice.'

10.15 French

'Guess who?' I whisper to Dougie as I'm perfecting my cartoon of S. Doyle, the two-faced arsehole. It's not bad. One cheek is the smarmy-looking face that people get taken in by. The other is the sly, sadistic psycho he really is. I nudge Dougie and slide it towards him.

'Looks like a bum with an expensive haircut,' he mutters.

I add two hairy legs and some other body parts. Dougie starts to snigger. He's getting out of control, making snorting noises and vibrating. I draw a speech bubble coming out of Doyle's bum and I write, *I am a load of shi—*

Dougie elbows me in the ribs and his eyes signal

behind us. I look round to see old Creepy-Crawley looking with interest over my shoulder.

'And who is this supposed to represent, might I ask?'

'Er – it's not you, Mr Crawley. It's er – something I just made up.'

'No – I see that now.'

He picks it up and peers at it closely, stroking his beard. 'Dear me. Whoever it is seems to be in need of urgent medical attention, if not surgery. This poor individual merits an entry in *The Guinness Book of Records*. No doubt about it.'

Everyone's watching. Kids crowd round us, craning their necks to see what he's looking at.

'Are we planning on a career as a satirical cartoonist, then Ed? Why is it that boys have such an obsession with genitalia and excrement, eh?' he asks the class. 'Usually they grow out of it by the age of three or four. But you, Ed – your development seems to be sadly retarded.' He slips my cartoon into his top pocket. 'I'll keep this if I may – in exchange for this.' He hands me a yellow card. 'Which tutor group are you in?'

'9H, Mr Crawley.'

'You are a severe disappointment to me, Ed. Maybe I'd have been prepared to excuse you, if you had made some attempt to use French.'

Stupid yellow card. As if I care? Whoa! – two more yellow cards and then a red one! And – oh help! A detention! A few days ago, that would have bothered me. Now, it's almost funny.

10.35 Break

'Look there – see them?' mutters Dougie.

I follow his glance to see two mean-looking big lads leaning against the wall.

'They're two of the apes that got me in the bogs.'

'Where's Ryan, then?' asks Carl.

'Dunno.'

'Oi! Ed!' Ali Patel comes jogging over. 'Mr Hargreaves wants to see you. Now – staffroom!'

■

'What's going on?' asks Mr Hargreaves, taking a sip from his mug of tea.

We're standing in the corridor up from the school office. A couple of kids waiting outside are giving me a right eyeballing.

'Er – what d'you mean?'

'I think you know what I mean,' he says.

He can't have found out, can he? What am I gonna say? I can't grass . . . But if he does know . . . My insides are swirling: panic – then relief – panic – panic – relief – panic—

He's taking something from his pocket. It's – it's – a yellow slip. 'From Mr Crawley,' he announces. He holds it up in front of my face. 'What does it say, Ed?'

I stare at it.

'Read it out, lad.'

'Er – for time-wasting time in French and confiscation of an obscene drawing.'

'That's Number One,' he sighs. 'And this is Number Two.' He opens another note. 'A request from Mr Day for your homework – which should have been in his pigeonhole first thing. Not too happy with you, is he? A bit of a slacker of late, a bit of a joker, he tells me. All coming back now, is it?'

There's something caught in his teeth – and dandruff on his jacket.

English homework. I forgot. Didn't I?

'Well? Do I get an answer? I hope you've got some very good reasons.'

Yes, Mr Hargreaves. You see I'm going to get slaughtered on Friday – there didn't seem much point.

'I know. I'm sorry, I forgot my English book. It's at home.'

'I'll tell Mr Day you'll deliver it first thing tomorrow, then. And what about the other matter?'

'It was only a cartoon – a joke, Mr Hargreaves.'

'Mmmm – well if you must indulge in smutty cartoons, do them in your own time, eh? OK,' he sighs. 'You can go.'

∎

May as well make my way to Maths – bell's gonna go any sec anyway – and I need a bit of space.

'Hey, Ed!' Glenn Barnes catches me up. 'What's this I hear about a punch up?'

'What?'

'You know. You and Doyle?'

'What're you talking about?'

'Ryan says Doyle's after you.'

'Ryan?'

'Yeah.'

'Ryan told you that?'

'Yeah. On Friday, he says.'

What's Ryan playing at? Just wait till I find him.

'Well? Is it true?' asks Glenn.

'It's news to me.'

'Not that I believed him,' he shrugs.

12.05 Lunchtime

'I can't believe you did that! You total air-brain! Are you stupid, Ryan! What're you doing, telling everyone!'

'It's for a reason. I've had this idea . . .'

'What? What? I don't believe this!'

Ryan flaps his arms and blinks at me. 'Look, I didn't start this! You did!'

I can't be bothered with him. I walk off. Carl and Dougie are coming towards me. I tell them about Ryan's big mouth.

'Whaaat?' they bleat together.

Ryan joins us.

Carl glares at him. 'Man – what you do that for! It makes us *all* look like jerks! You need your head seein' to! Jeee-sus!' He shakes his head in despair.

'That is so-o-o-o dumb,' sighs Dougie. 'Major dumb. Dumb-dumb-dumb!'

'Why's everyone blaming me?' squeals Ryan. 'Dougie! You got done yesterday! I got done to today! All down to Ed!' He glares at me. 'It's him you should be mouthing off at! Anyway, you'll thank me later – when you've calmed down a bit! I've got an idea which . . .'

I don't want to hear.

Carl comes after me. 'Where you goin'?'

I keep walking. Find myself heading for the old Special Needs mobile. It's out of use, out of bounds and out of sight, in a dip between the school buildings and a playing field, which is why it's supposed to be out of bounds. To get there you have to pass a staffroom window, which means you have to crouch down and practically crawl on all fours to get past. As I reach the slope to the dip I glance over my shoulder to see Carl and Dougie following me, scuttling under the window. It feels like I'm leading an SAS raiding party or something. I check behind the mobile that there aren't any dopeheads about – it used to be a fave place for them. It's freezing here. I'm zipping up my jacket when Carl and Dougie come round the corner – and, I can't believe it – they're followed by Ryan.

No one says anything for a bit. I squat down on to the low wall. Dougie and Carl join me. We all look up at Ryan.

'Well?' scowls Dougie. 'You gonna tell us, then – this dumb idea, of yours?'

'It better be good!' warns Carl, pulling up his collar. 'It just better be good.'

'Look, just remember I didn't start this,' Ryan blusters. He fumbles in his jacket, takes out a packet of ciggies and lights up. He squats down opposite us. 'Anyway, it was bound to get out. Sooner or later,' he says.

'No it wasn't! I cannot believe you did that! I look like a total idiot. I've had kids telling me I'm gonna die, giving me advice. Andrew Paisley reckons I should tell Mr Hargreaves. And I don't want to imagine what it's going to be like when Sonya and Brett and that lot get on to me! What am I s'posed to say?'

'That's funny, that is! You've *always* got something to say. That's the problem.'

'If you two don't shut up, I'm going,' says Carl.

'OK, OK!' Ryan flaps. 'I'm sorreee! But if you'd just listen a sec, please . . .'

'Get on with it then!' yells Carl.

'Right,' Ryan begins. He takes a drag. 'Something's going to happen on Friday, right? And the message I got is that there's gonna be some sort of – ' he shrugs, ' – bundle, doing over, whatever, right? Now there's a lot of kids who'd like to see Doyle lose—'

'It won't be Doyle,' Dougie cuts in, blowing on to his hands. 'Doyle won't get himself dirty – probably won't even be there. No way.'

Ryan is flustered. He's twitching all over the place.

'OK, OK! But *whoever* it is – there's loads of kids who would love to see Ed come out of this a winner, right?'

Dougie laughs. 'No chance, no chance.' He looks at me. 'Sorry mate. But it's true, isn't it?'

'Yeah. But they don't *know* that, do they?' Ryan blurts. 'For all they know, Ed here could be a black-belt karate champion!'

Dougie snorts. Carl sighs and rolls his eyes.

'Problem is,' says Ryan, 'those kids – the ones on your side – they keep a low profile. They don't want trouble. They keep quiet. Remember all those kids that laughed? Remembered how you said you'd never forget the look on Doyle's face, Carl? Lots of kids think the same. We ought to be using that. Now, the way I see it, if Ed knew there were loads of kids rooting for him, wanting him to win, it would help a bit wouldn't it? Build up his confidence like. And then he—'

'I'm still here, Ryan,' I interrupt. 'P'raps you can include me in this?'

He leans forward on his knees, looking at me. 'Look, I still think what you did was dumb. But we're stuck with it. So what are we gonna do about it, eh? They think we're *all* jerks! All I'm saying is, it's all in the mind, innit? Think like a loser and you'll be a loser, right?' He taps his head.

What's he going on about? He keeps glancing at Carl and Dougie and nodding, like he wants their approval.

'So, first you've got to think positive. Second, we build you up into some sort of mini-hero. Doyle won't like that. Especially if it looks like loads of kids are on *your* side, wanting you to get the better of him—'

'You're mad! A mini-hero? What d'you think I am, Super-Ted or something? Bug off, Ryan! I'm not going to get the better of anyone! I'm gonna get done, that's what! Whoever it is – I am gonna get done. That's bad enough. But now the *whole world* knows I'm gonna get done!'

'Let me speak, willya!' Ryan squeals.

Dougie has his head in his hands.

'This four days stuff – it's all about making you suffer, isn't it?' Ryan goes on. 'Spinning the torture out. That's what they're getting pleasure from. It's not just you. It's all of us. That's what you were saying, Carl, last night, remember? You said we mustn't let them see it's getting to us, because that's just what Doyle wants. Well, I'm agreeing with you. And I'm saying we should try playing him at his own game and—'

'Ryan – get real, will you?' I say.

'No, hang about,' Carl sighs. 'Maybe Ryan's got a point, sort of. Just sitting around waiting is the worst thing we can do. Especially after what they did to Dougie. Even more now that the news has leaked out – thanks to you, Ryan! We have to do *something*. Find a way of putting a spin on things. I dunno what but—'

'I don't get it,' shrugs Dougie.

Neither do I. It's my head that's spinning. My guts are churning. I am totally wound up.

'They think you're going to be a pushover. They think we're all pushovers!' Ryan scowls. 'Aw – I'd love to get back at them. Show them none of us are pushovers! It's diabolical what Doyle gets away with – it's diabolical!'

'Look,' says Carl, spreading his hands. 'Maybe – if we just stay cool, act like we know something they don't, well that might ruffle them a bit. Then like Ryan says, we could get them to see loads of kids *are* on your side. That *could* be interesting. Hey! It's like David and Goliath, innit? That's not a bad idea. At least we'll be doing something. Better than just waiting for stuff to happen to us.'

Suddenly, Ryan's grinning, nodding his head off. 'See?' he keeps saying. 'See? Can't do any harm, can it?'

'Pro-active,' says Dougie.

'What?' says Ryan.

'Pro-active,' shrugs Dougie, shoving his hands under his arms. 'Being in control – taking charge. My mum's always going on about being pro-active, in't she, Carl?'

'Yeah. Has him down for first black prime-minister. Prime suspect, more like.'

'What? What are you talking about? I don't get it,' I say.

Ryan gets to his feet and paces up and down. 'Look, Ed! What you got to remember – it's all up here.' He taps his head. 'In the mind. Positive thinking. That's what it is – wait! Wait! I've got it! . . .' He feels in his pocket, takes out a pound coin and carefully places it on the wall. 'I am going to bet one pound – no make it two –' he adds another coin and looks at Carl and Dougie, 'I am prepared to bet that Ed will win the fight.'

We all stare at him, like he's flipped. He blinks back at us.

'No chance, mate.' Dougie shakes his head. 'Sorry an' all that Ed, but no chance.'

'OK – three pounds,' says Ryan. 'No, on third thoughts – a fiver.' He roots in his pockets – brings out a handful of pennies. 'Well, I'll owe the kitty two pounds, OK?'

'No way! You cannot seriously think that he can win?' Dougie's voice goes into a squeal.

'You are seriously crazy, Ryan,' says Carl shaking his head.

'Stranger things have happened,' he blinks.

'It ain't gonna happen. No way,' Dougie huffs.

'Listen!' says Ryan flapping his arms. 'A bloke with no legs climbed Everest! I saw him on telly. Everyone said it was impossible! Said he couldn't do it! But he did!'

Carl jokes, 'Weh-heh! Can you just imagine it if you *did* win? Man, that would be something!'

'I s'pose – if you put up a fight like, even if you got beat, you'd get some respect.' Dougie shrugs. 'Yeah. You'd be a sort of hero. It's a ginormous *IF* though.'

'See?' says Ryan. 'See? It's happening already! It's changed from an "*ain't gonna happen*" to an "*if*". Psychological innit? "*If*" is good, "*if*" is. "*If*" means you got a chance. Better than "*no chance*". If we can build Ed up – well, it won't do any harm. It'll give Doyle and his mates something to think about. From now on you don't even *think* about losing!'

It's like he's a different person. Like he really believes this crazy idea will work.

'Ryan,' I groan. 'It's *never* gonna work. Stuff psychology! Stuff "*if*". It's all hot air! What I really need is a body transplant! Mike Tyson – he'll do.'

'Wait a mo,' says Carl. 'I get what Ryan's saying – kind of. It's not just about muscle, is it? It's got a lot to do with – well, self-belief and willpower and skill. No good telling yourself you *can't* do stuff. You got to believe in yourself. And there's stuff you could learn. Sticking your fingers up an attacker's nose – that's a good one. Simone learnt that at a self-defence class. She tried that one on me.'

'Ugh! That's disgusting, that is,' says Dougie.

'It works, believe me it works,' Carl nods. 'You can't

move. There's loads of simple stuff like that. Can't do any harm, can it?'

'Kick him in the goolies,' says Ryan, aiming a kick at an invisible opponent.

I stand up. 'Oh yeah! It's so *easy* to talk! But it's *me* who's going to have to do it, isn't it? I don't even know where! Or who! Or anything! And I know bog all about how to fight. You're talking total rubbish!'

'Wait!' Dougie looks at Carl. 'Carl – what about Elvira?'

'Yeah, Elvira. Elvira could be useful,' Carl nods.

'Reckon we could all do with some advice from Elvira,' Dougie sighs.

'I can look after myself,' says Carl. 'But it's not a bad idea.'

'Who's Elvira?' I want to know.

'Raymond's girlfriend,' says Dougie.

'Who's Raymond?' asks Ryan.

'Our cousin,' says Carl. 'Elvira teaches martial arts and stuff. Ray's always goin' on about Elvira.'

'You're mad! It's Tuesday! I've only got till Friday! I can't learn that stuff in two days!'

'That's bad attitude, Ed,' says Carl. 'You gotta *believe* you can.'

'OK, let's have your money,' says Ryan holding out his hand. 'Come on Dougie.'

'What? But . . .'

'Faith,' says Ryan. 'You gotta show faith in Ed. Build

his confidence up. You too, Carl.'

He grabs his bag and tugs out his rough book, balances it on his knee and takes out a pen. He holds out his hand to Dougie.

'Come on then. How much you gonna bet on Ed winning?'

Dougie groans, 'I dunno – I'm not sure this'll work.'

'Well, if you can't count on yer mates, who can you count on?' Ryan snorts. 'Right, I'll put myself down, then – five quid. Don't worry, Ed, you can tell who your real friends are. No problem. You'll soon find others.'

'You're going to run a book on me?' I blink.

'Yep.'

'You are joking,' says Dougie. 'What odds?'

Ryan stares at the ground in concentration. 'Twenty to one on Ed winning,' he says eventually.

'Twenty to one! Jeez!' stares Dougie.

'And your one pound stake back.'

'Why didn't you say?' Dougie says. 'So if I bet a quid and Ed wins – I get twenty quid back? Can't lose. Worth a quid just for the buzz of getting up Doyle's nose.'

Dougie digs into his pockets and hands over a pound coin.

'Dougie, one pound,' Ryan writes. 'Is that all?'

'Wait – make it two pound fifty,' says Dougie, and he

counts out a handful of coins. 'You win, Ed, and I get fifty quid!'

'Yeah, same for me, then,' nods Carl.

I'm feeling a big panic coming on. 'Look, hang about. Hang about! Let me get this straight. If I win, you have to pay everyone back the money they bet? Plus twenty times the bet? Where you gonna get all the money?'

Ryan blinks. Then grins at me. 'See? You said, "If I win." You're thinking like a winner already! Brilliant or what? Look – don't worry about it.'

'Hold on. Ed's gotta point there,' Dougie says. 'If he *does* win, you're gonna have to find a lotta loot to pay people out. I don't understand. Where *are* you gonna find that sort of dosh to pay 'em, eh? It ain't possible!'

Ryan sighs. 'Right – let's get real, here. Ed's not gonna win, is he? But that's not the point is it? The point is—'

'You mean me and Carl have just given you five quid for nothing!' Dougie blinks.

'Oh thanks, Ryan,' I say. 'Great build up. Then . . . plop!'

'Look,' he shrugs, 'maybe you'll get lucky. But this is about getting back at Doyle and the rest. It's about face. It's about front. It's about getting kids to back you. Like Carl said – David and Goliath, ain't it? Whatever happens, everyone will *want* it to be you. And either way, *you win.*'

'What? How d'you make that out?' I ask.

'Well, if you win – well you *win*, don't you? Can't ask for more than that! If you don't – you get respect. And –' he stops and thinks '– and you get a cut of the takings!' he announces.

'I do? How much?'

He stares thoughtfully down at this feet. 'Ten per cent,' he says eventually.

'Only ten per cent? Get off!' says Carl.

'He ought to get half – minimum,' says Dougie.

'Half? Seventy-five per cent more like. It's only fair,' adds Carl.

'Look!' explodes Ryan. 'I'm taking a gamble here! I've gotta get something out of it!'

'A gamble? You just told me I couldn't win!'

'Well – there you go! You're starting to have faith in yourself, aren't you?'

'What?' *I'm confused. And sick with worry.*

12.45

'He's gonna ring us back,' says Dougie, slipping his mobile back into his pocket. 'Raymond's gonna call Elvira on her mobile. He wanted to know what it was all about. I said it was urgent – that you're being menaced by a gang from another school.'

'Yeah – we all heard,' I sigh. 'Specially the bit about how nasty they are and how feeble I am.'

'She's good is she, this Elvira?' asks Ryan.

Dougie shrugs. 'Raymond rates her. Haven't met her yet, have we, Carl?'

'Anyone want my sandwiches?' I offer.

I haul my bag on to the wall. All this talk about fighting – I feel like I'm gonna throw up. It's like they're talking about someone else. Oh, no – how did *this* get into my bag? A long white envelope. Just like the one Ryan got. I don't want this.

For the Attention of Edwin Tully

'That's not what I think it is, is it?' sighs Carl.

'You gotta open it. Want me to do it?' offers Dougie.

I make myself tear it open. Another old, used school letter, thanking parents for all their help at the autumn fair and telling them that Mrs Slattery won the Name The Teddy competition and Tabitha Potts won The Owner Who Looks Most Like Their Pet one. *Why am I bothering to read this?*

Carl takes it out of my hand. He turns it over and stares down at it. 'Doesn't make any sense,' he says. He holds it up. It says:

DO NOT PASS GO

'Don't worry,' sighs Dougie. 'We'll find out soon enough.' He stands up. 'Anyone wanna accompany me to the bogs, then?'

'Look – I'm gonna see if I can get any more takers,' says Ryan.

■

I'm the first one to see it. The word GO has been scrawled in chalk on to the door to the boys' bogs. Is this the GO I'm not allowed to pass? Suddenly I have the urgent need to go.

'Tossers!' says Dougie when he sees it. 'Who do they think they are, eh?'

A couple of kids come out – they don't seem bothered about anything.

'Maybe it's just a wind-up,' says Carl. 'What d'you think?'

He pushes the door open and we peer in. Someone is standing at the urinal. There's a flushing from one of the cubicles and Ali Patel's brother Mo comes out. Carl peers under the cubical doors. 'Nothing,' he shrugs.

Dougie heads for the urinal. I shoot into a cubicle – slam the door shut. Thinking about fighting has turned my insides to liquid. *Quick! Quick!*

'Have you seen *this?*' Carl's voice.

A groan. 'There's more here.' Dougie's voice. 'And on that wall.'

I think I know what they're talking about – I've just see what's on the back of the door.

E.S. IS A QUEER!
KILL THE POOFTERS!
RID THE WORLD OF FAGGOTS!

Crash!

What's that? Like the door smashing open – what's happening? . . .

'Out! You! Out! All of yer! Out!'

Who is that?

'What?'

That's Dougie's voice.

'You deaf? Move it!'

'Get off willya!'

Dougie again. Scuffling noises – muffled voices – grunts . . . My insides are exploding. This is a nightmare – and I'm stuck on the bog.

'Woo-hoo! Anyone home?'

Laughter.

'Oi! Queer boy! You got visitors!'

How many of them? Quick – quick – paper! Paper! Hurry up. PLEASE, PLEASE – just let me finish! Hurry – hurry . . .

'He's in this one.'

They're here. Just the door between us—

Bang! Crash! Bash!

They're kicking the door in! They're kicking the door in . . .

What? It's gone quiet . . .

Sniggering – really close . . .

'We're coming to get you!'

'Frigging hell – it stinks in here! Don't have to look for him! Can sniff him out!'

Crash! – from the next cubicle.

Crash! – the other side. What are they doing?

Pull your trousers up! Quick! Quick!

Oh God – they're climbing up, aren't they? Where's my zip? Where's my zip?

'Well, look! If it isn't Little Miss Tinkerbelle.'

A face leering down at me from the side – another two pop up . . .

'Who's been a naughty boy, then?'

'He didn't read the sign, did he?'

'We'd better teach him a lesson, hadn't we?'

It's the two apes that got Dougie – and another one. Why doesn't someone come in? Please – someone come in! Please, please . . .

14.16 Home

The phone's ringing. The answer tape clicks on. '*We cannot get to the phone right now. Please leave your message after the tone.*' Click.

'Ed – it's me, Carl. Ed? Are you there? Ed? I don't think he's in . . .'

I drag myself off the sofa and pick it up. 'Yeah – I'm here.'

'You OK, man?'

'Yeah.'

'Hell – we've been worried sick! You just vanished. What happened there?'

'Look – I don't wanna talk about it right now, I'm not feeling—'

'You bunked off, then?'

'No – yeah. Got taken bad – my stomach. It's official. Reported it to the school office.'

'Hang about, Ed . . . Says he's ill,' he tells someone.

'Hey, Ed, it's me – Dougie. It's all set up.'

'What is?'

'With Elvira, right? Five o'clock at the Respect Academy, right? Know where that is? Near the station – round the corner from the Speedo Pizza place, right?'

'No. Look—'

'You gotta make it, Ed. Don't waste it. We're all going. Can't lose anything, can you?'

'I dunno – I'm feeling bad—'

'You ought to try – honest, Ed. You'll feel worse if you don't. Respect Academy, right? Hold on . . .'

'Hey, Ed. Listen. It's me, Ryan. I've got thirty-seven bets so far. Loads of kids are backing you. Five o'clock, right?'

'Ed – it's Carl again. You be there.'

16.55 The Respect Academy of Martial Arts

What am I doing here? It stinks of sweat and disinfectant. This is stupid. I left home early so there was no chance of bumping into anyone going home from school. Didn't want to be caught at home when Ellie got back from college either. Can't be worse than sitting at home going over and over what happened, can it? All the way here – looking over my shoulder. Trying to think of some way out.

Here come Carl and Dougie through the doors.

'OK?' says Carl.

I shrug.

'We couldn't do anything,' he says. 'There were two more of them on the outside of the bogs, stopping anyone going in.'

'Where's Ryan?'

'Went home first,' says Dougie.

Carl stares at me. 'What happened, then?'

A bloke comes out of a door with some posters in his hand. ' 'Scuse me,' he grunts, nodding at the wall behind us.

We move out of the way for him to stick them up. The lobby we're standing in is covered with posters. Men in white pyjama suits, frozen in poses – fists closed, fists open like blades. Another is flying horizontally through the air, feet-first at his opponent. Men clashing sticks. Men in black – wearing helmets that look like cages, brandishing deadly-looking swords. Stuff I've only seen in Kung Fu films.

'Here's Ryan,' nods Dougie. 'Come on. She said Room 2D – it's on the second floor.'

'Sorry – missed the bus,' Ryan pants.

■

Elvira is not like I expected. She's tiny. Like a doll.

Wearing this tight pink leotard with purple leggings, showing off all her curves. Her head's a mass of shiny black ropes.

Carl's eyes are on stalks. Ryan's grinning. Dougie just blinks.

This is mad. What am I doing here? I haven't come for Bums and Tums *that my mum goes to.*

'Carl, right?' Elvira smiles. 'And Dougie, yeah? Nice to meet you – Raymond's cousins, right?'

She turns to me. 'And . . . ?'

'Ed.'

'Ryan,' blinks Ryan.

'OK,' she says. 'You want some help with taking care of yourselves, right?'

Carl shrugs and nods in my direction. 'Ed's getting some harassment. I'll just watch, thanks.' He heads for a bench.

'Look – I'm not gonna hurt you!' she laughs. 'Come back here!' She waves him back. 'I need you to work in pairs in a bit.'

Carl sheepishly makes his way back.

She looks at me. 'OK – I'm not going to ask questions, but if any of you *are* having trouble on a regular basis, you have to report it, right?'

We all nod in agreement.

She looks up at the clock. 'I've only got about half an hour. I can't do much. All I can do is run quickly through some basics, right?'

We nod again.

'But you really ought to come along to one of my classes – there's leaflets over there. I do several under-sixteens classes. They can really do a lot for your confidence. Right – I'll take you through some techniques that can get you out of a tight spot. After that, it's about practice. Practice, practice practice.' She taps her fist against her palm with each word. 'So that's down to you,' she points.

She holds up her forefinger. 'Rule Number One: don't take risks. That means avoid being alone. Stick with a group. Yeah?'

We nod again. We're turning into Noddy quads.

She holds up two fingers. 'Rule Two: don't go looking for trouble.'

'Huh!' says Ryan, glancing at me. 'You can say that again.'

'And rule Number Three: don't start thinking like a victim. *Do* something.'

'See?' Ryan signals to me.

'Like you're here – you're *doing* something,' she nods. 'So that's good. You've made a start.'

I feel empty. Like I'm not really here. What *am* I doing here? I wanna be back to Monday, back to the car park. Only this time I'll just walk away.

Carl's looking round the room, like this is all kids' stuff and he's just come along to keep an eye on things.

'So – don't *think* like a victim – and more importantly,

don't *look* like a victim. No nervous fidgeting, avoiding eye-contact – that sort of thing.'

Ryan starts shuffling his feet.

'If someone has a go at you, it's important to try and look *confident*.' She walks towards Carl. 'Just like Carl here.' He grins at her. 'Nice and upright. Relaxed but assertive. Unruffled. Calm. Steady eye-contact – but not aggressive.'

She gets behind Ryan, straightens his shoulders and lifts his chin. He grins idiotically and goes bright pink.

I know all this. And I know I need more than steady eye-contact! This is pathetic.

She carries on walking round us. 'If someone *does* have a go at you, the worst thing you can do is go into frozen-rabbit syndrome. So keep calm – but *don't* freeze! Your first resort – *always* – is to get away. Run! Get away! Your *last* resort – only if you have *no* other choice – is to get physical.'

Ryan sniggers.

'And this is the time when you use the magic ingredient. Any guesses? What's the magic ingredient, eh?'

I want to say something stupid, like, *The power of invisibility*, or *The Starship Enterprise* – so all I have to say is *Beam me up, Scottie*.

'Kick him in the goolies,' says Ryan.

'Yeah – maybe,' she nods. 'But basically, your magic ingredient is *surprise*. It allows *you* – the victim – to take the initiative. Most attackers do not expect you to resist. *Surprise* is your biggest weapon!'

So on Friday when I meet up with whoever is gonna do me – I jump out and say BOO! do I?

She puts her hands on her hips. She's got a really good body, even though she's so tiny. But she doesn't have a clue. How's this going to help?

'OK,' she says. 'So let's imagine – you're walking home and someone leaps out at you. How do you *feel*?'

No one says anything.

'Come on! He's got a knife! He looks crazy! How do you feel?'

This is a waste of time.

'Dougie?'

'Terrified,' he shrugs.

She nods. 'Yup. Fear. You feel fear. Even the best-trained commando feels fear. Fear can numb you. Fear can make you freeze. Fear can make you panic. And if you let your fear do that – you become a victim.'

Is this supposed to make me feel better?

'It's perfectly normal,' she goes on. 'You're afraid because you feel helpless and don't know what to do.'

Too right.

'So what I'm gonna do is teach you a few very simple, easy-to-learn techniques that'll give you a bit of confidence.'

Oh yeah? I'm gonna become Superman, am I?

'What you've got to remember,' she says, 'is that even a highly-trained commando isn't Superman.'

Is she reading my mind?

'Under attack, he feels the same sickening fear as you.'

No he doesn't. A commando would have a ruddy great machine gun and hand grenades. Not to mention body armour. I'd feel like Superman with that lot. No fear. Doyle can kiss my butt with that lot on.

She pauses and looks at each one of us in turn. 'The difference is that his training has given him the confidence not to panic. And to channel his fear into anger against his attackers. That's what you have to learn to do. It's *attitude*, right? Another magic ingredient, right?'

'See?' Ryan nods. 'That's what I was saying, remember?'

'Attitude is very important,' says Elvira. 'But it's not enough on its own. It comes with the confidence of knowing what to do.'

She looks round at us. 'Right – I need a volunteer. Ryan? Kick-'em-in-the-goolies-man? You'll do.'

'What? I reckon it should be Ed first. Oh – OK,' he groans.

'Over here on the mats,' she says. 'Stand there, Ryan. Now, I want you to show me how to kick someone in the goolies – as hard as you can.'

He grins round at us then demonstrates a powerful kick.

Will someone please tell me – what is the point of this?

'Good,' she says. 'And again – even harder.'

He kicks again.

She positions herself in front of him. 'Now, forget it's me. I'm a nasty, violent thug and I'm gonna turn you into mincemeat, right? So I want you to kick me – just like you did there – only harder.'

Ryan screws up his face. 'Are you sure about this?'

She nods. 'Come on. Kick as hard as you can.'

He steps back and takes a powerful kick. Next thing she's got him by the ankle, pushes her hand under his chin, and he's thrown off balance, flat on his back – her leg pinning his head to the floor, with his arm caught in there somewhere in a lock.

'Aaaah – I – I can't m-move – I can't move,' he's stuttering.

'I did that very slowly – making sure he didn't fall too hard or hurt himself,' she says. 'The real thing would have been faster. Now if I wanted,' she says calmly, 'I could apply a *very* painful armlock here. I could break his arm if it was a serious assault – and that would put him out of action.' She releases her hold on him. He sits up.

'That was scary,' he puffs. 'That was well impressive.'

She beckons Carl over. 'OK – Carl. Stand there, will you?'

He steps forward, hands in pockets, grinning.

She moves back. 'OK Carl – I want you to take a punch at me.'

'What? No way!' he grins. 'I can't do that!'

'OK,' she shrugs. 'Try and make a grab for me.'

He makes a playful grab.

'Come on! Come on!' she goads, dodging away. 'Just try and get me! Bet you can't! You're not even trying! Come on!'

He makes a feeble lunge. Instantly she grabs his arm, twists round with her back to him and tugs him over her shoulder. He's flat on his back and she's got him pinned.

'Aaaagh! Aaaagh!' He's half moaning, half laughing.

'Don't be such a baby,' she says. 'I'm not hurting you. Now try and get out of it.'

'I can't – I can't – it hurts if I move,' he winces.

'That's an entangled armlock,' she announces, standing up.

Carl blinks and shakes his head. He gets to his feet and shrugs and grins. 'How d'you do that? It ain't possible!'

'It's simple when you know how. Broken down – it's about evading your attacker, defending yourself, knowing the vulnerable body targets, and how to use your own body weapons.'

What? I'm never gonna take all this in. By the look on the others' faces, they're thinking the same thing.

'Don't worry about that for now,' she says. 'You'll get the hang of it when you start to practise. You need to practise over and over – so you don't even have to think about it. So your body goes on auto-pilot.'

She looks hard at me. 'Now the point of that was to show you that *size* is not essential. And it's not about strength either.'

She is *a mind-reader. She's definitely a mind-reader*.

She turns to Carl. 'How much do you weigh, Carl?'

'About ten and a half,' he shrugs.

'I'm just over seven stone,' she says. 'So remember, it's *not* the size of the dog in the fight that counts – it's the size of the fight in the dog.'

She calls me over and shows me some stuff. And after a couple of practices, somehow I manage to throw Carl over my shoulder – and hold him pinned to the ground. OK, he let me – but it's a start.

'Well done,' she says. 'Now you can see. It's about mastering some simple self-defence skills – and the confidence that comes with them. Have I convinced you? Right, let's start. Pair up.'

17.37 Respect Academy Locker Room

'I'm sweating – look at my shirt.' Ryan points.

Dougie wriggles his nose. 'Put it away, Ry! I can smell you from here!'

'Where we gonna practise, then?' I ask.

'Everyone come round to mine. We can use the den

again – I'll make some space,' says Carl, splashing his face. He looks at his watch. 'About seven? No make it a bit later – quarter past, OK?'

'Oi, Ed,' says Ryan. He tugs something from his back pocket. 'There you go!'

It's a torn-out page from his rough book. On it is scrawled £57.50.

'That's how much I've taken so far – and that's only for starters. All those kids are on your side, Ed.'

Dougie's phone bleeps. He takes it from his pocket. 'Ain't mine,' he says, frowning down at it.

'It's coming from you, Ryan!' I say.

'What? Oh yeah.' He reaches into his pocket and takes out a mobile.

'Didn't know you had a mobile,' says Dougie.

Ryan turns his back on us and moves away.

'Yeah?' I hear him say. 'No – it's a bit difficult. OK, OK.'

'When did you get that?' asks Carl.

'Borrowed it from my sister. Security, isn't it? Anyhow, she wants it back – I gotta go. Seeya later.'

'Pinched it, more like,' says Dougie, as the door closes behind Ryan. 'Hey,' Dougie says. 'I am never gonna forget seeing that little Elvira throwing you like that, Carl. You gotta admit, Ed, if she can do it –' he shrugs, '– then we all can, right? Including you.'

Carl looks at me. 'You're looking a bit better.'

I shrug. It doesn't seem possible, but yeah – I *do* feel better. Well, better than when I arrived here. I mean, Dougie's right, if a little body like Elvira can do it, I can, can't I? I toppled Carl. I got Ryan in a headlock. I know it wasn't the real thing. But seeing that – well *anyone* can, can't they? Got to practise. Got to practise, practise, practise. Every spare moment. Practise.

'That was stonking, that was,' Dougie says. 'Wish I'd known that stuff before they got me in the bogs. I might give her classes a go, seriously.'

Carl says, 'You haven't told us what happened in the bogs.'

Don't want to be reminded. Just when I'd pushed it to the back of my mind. But I tell them. How those pigs filled the basin with water and held my face under. How they tipped my bag all over the floor. Helped themselves to my calculator and CD-player, the one that cost all my birthday money to buy.

'Oh yeah – and they took all my money too. Had to walk all the way home.'

I don't tell them about the things they made me recite, about what 'gay boys' do. And I don't tell them that I got caught short and had to wash my pants when I got home. I'm not even going to think about that. All I'm going to think about is the shock on their faces as I aim a deadly kick at Sharples's groin, spin round with an elbow thrust into Zimmer's solar plexus, and finish with a double finger-poke in Doyle's eyes and a shoulder throw with a bone-breaking arm pin on the ground.

18.10

I'm sitting on the bus, practising my body weapons on the vulnerable body targets of Doyle, Sharples and Zimmer. When they're begging for mercy I start on Brett, Clive and Jason—

'Oh, hi!'

I glance up to see Caitlin looking down at me.

'All right if I sit here?'

'Yeah. Help yourself.'

'You weren't in English this afternoon.'

'Had to go to the dentist. A filling.' I point to a tooth.

'I haven't got any. Fillings – not teeth,' she grins. 'Should have loads. I'm mad about chocolate. It drives my mum nuts. She's a dental hygienist, see.'

'Right.'

She folds and unfolds her ticket. She looks different out of uniform. Much older. Girls usually do. I look out of the window. It's too dark to see properly. At our age girls can easily look twenty. I could never pass for twenty. I can see her reflection. It's the make-up that makes her look older. All that black round her eyes. And she's got these coloured tassels in her hair. She smells nice too.

'Is it true?' she asks. 'What they're saying?'

'What?'

'That there's going to be a fight – with you and Stuart

Doyle. I heard that friend of yours, the freckly one—'

'Ryan?'

'Yeah, Ryan. Well he's taking bets, isn't he? So it must be true?'

'Dunno,' I say.

'But you must know!'

'It could all be part of a wind-up, for all I know.' I look out of the window again, trying to think of something to change the subject.

'Anyway, I can't stand those three – so sickeningly smug. Specially that Stuart Doyle. He's a real slimeball. Really fancies himself. Can't stand his type. The way some girls drool about him! Ugh – I don't get it! I'm a very good judge of character too – honest. Go on, test me.'

'OK, what about me, then?'

'Mmmm,' she goes. 'Impetuous. Funny—'

'Funny? What sort of funny?'

'Funny-ha-ha. Like Doyle's brain being the size of a pea.' She holds up her fingers and laughs. 'And stupid – for saying it to someone like *him*. And brave – for saying it to someone like *him*. And kind too.' She goes all serious. 'For stopping that cruel, vicious, nasty, torture on that poor boy. Every day,' she says. 'Every day. I couldn't bear to watch. It was too awful. What must he have been going through?'

Her eyes are blue. Bright blue. Bright blue eyes and shiny black hair.

'We used to go around together.'

'Is that why you did it – stuck up for him?'

'S'pose.'

'What happened, then? Why d'you two split?' she asks.

'Dunno – just one of those things,' I shrug.

'*Is* he gay – like kids say?'

I make a *who knows?* face.

'You're not really going to fight him, are you?'

I shrug again.

'You ought to tell someone.'

I snort a laugh. It's not even worth trying to explain.

'Couldn't you tell them about Lester? You could tell Head of Year, Mr Sturgeon.'

'Look – it's been going on for ages. Lester could have reported it any time. He chose not to. Up to him isn't it? Anyway, if teachers start asking questions everyone clams up. He'd end up looking like some little kid telling tales. They'd give him an even harder time.'

'There has to be some way, though,' she says.

18.55 Home

'How's Lester these days?' asks Mum, clearing the table.

'What?'

'Bumped into Tina, his mum, in Sainsbury's. She's a bit worried about him – he doesn't appear to have many friends. Seems he spends all his time plugged into his music centre or his computer, and only talks in words of one syllable.'

'Reminds me of someone,' says Ellie without looking up from her magazine.

I shrug. 'How should I know?'

'Well, you used to be friends.'

'Yeah. *Used* to be.'

'You must see him around school though.'

'Look – I'm not his keeper, am I?'

'Oh well, just thought I'd ask,' she sighs. 'Never understood why you two broke up.' She looks at me like she's hoping for an answer.

'I'm off to Carl's, OK? Ouch!' I nearly trip over Jack who's scuttling round the kitchen in his baby-walker like a demented crab.

'Hold on! It's your turn to do the washing-up,' says Mum.

'But I'm late! I'm s'posed to be at Carl's by quarter past!'

'You should have thought of that before.'

'I'll do it if you give me a lift to Carl's, then.'

'That's blackmail. Anyway you've got time to do the washing-up – *and* bike to Carl's. *If* you get a move on.'

'Yeah,' says Ellie, flicking pages. 'Always making excuses. And you should have seen the mess when I got home, Mum. The bathroom was a tip. Can't even hang a towel up, poor feeble little brother. Disgusting curly little hairs in the shower! Why can't you clean up after yourself? And what's this sudden obsession with personal hygiene, anyway? Hey – I bet you've got a girlfriend. Hey, Mum! Guess what? My little brother's got a girlfriend!'

'Right! Fine! I'll go on my bike! *If* my batteries are working! *If* I can mend the puncture in time! *If* the roads aren't covered in ice and I don't skid into the back of an articulated lorry! *If* I can get the garage door to open more that six inches!'

'Your dad's promised he'll fix it next time he visits,' says Mum, lifting Jack out of his walker.

'What's her name then, Ed?' smirks Ellie.

'I'm off!'

'Strange name,' she grins. 'Is she Russian?'

'You do the washing-up first, Ed,' says Mum.

'Phone's ringing!' Ellie calls, as if we can't hear it. As if she can't just reach out an arm to lift it off the wall.

Mum sighs and picks it up. 'Hello. Yes, hold on . . .'

'It's for you,' she says holding it out to me.

'Hello?'

'Ed? It's me, Dougie. They got Carl.'

WEDNESDAY

They got Carl. I jolt awake. It all comes flooding back.

Must have slept then. Never thought I would. Must have fallen asleep thinking those words – they're recorded on to my brain.

They got Carl! Still can't take it in. They got him in Revolution Records as he walked out of the door. Got him when the alarm started bleeping and the shop assistants came running and grabbed him. Didn't matter that he hadn't a clue what was going on. Didn't matter that he'd got a receipt for a CD in his pocket. What mattered were the CDs that were hidden in the hood of his jacket. Didn't matter that he denied putting them there. Didn't matter that some sly sicko dropped them in and that Carl didn't realise. Didn't matter that he was set up. Only mattered that they were there. Over a hundred quid's worth. What matters is that they got him . . .

That horrible dream last night – all slowly coming back. I dreamed I get to school and there are these yellow arrows painted on the tarmac saying: THIS WAY TO FRIDAY. There's no one about – I'm terrified. But I start to follow the arrows. Then I think, *I know! I'll pretend I'm not me! I'll pretend I'm one of those who've come to beat me up!* And it seems like it's the most brilliant idea in the world. Why didn't I think if it before? So I stop and plaster my hair down and – now this is stupid – I roll up my trousers to my knees. Then I take off my jacket and turn it inside out and put it back on. *They're never gonna spot me now*, I'm thinking. I follow the arrows – and suddenly I'm behind The Wall of Death. It's dark and deserted. Well, that's what I think at first. Then dark shapes start emerging from behind the buildings. Loads of shadowy kids all coming for me. Can't make out any faces. And I can't move. Weird. Doyle, Zimmer, Sharples, Brett – couldn't see any of them. Just faceless people coming for me. Except for one face I *can* make out. And that's Carl.

08.45 Path at top of school car park

Ryan and me lean against the railings where the buses and kids come and go and teachers park their cars. Where there are plenty of people about. We watch the kids scrambling off the buses.

'Carl's mum and dad are doing their nut!'

We turn to see Dougie behind us.

'What? They don't think he really did nick that stuff?'

' 'Course not!' He glares. 'You've no idea, have you? Made to look like a criminal, he was! In front of everybody! The shop manager told him they'd heard it all before. Told him they're sick of kids – especially black kids – acting innocent and blaming other kids. He said a lot more too. Cussing him and stuff. The manager's denying all that now, though. And he made it clear they always prosecute.' He glowers at me then looks away.

'Does he have any idea who did it?' Ryan asks.

'Didn't *see* a thing. Didn't *feel* a thing. He's as mad as hell. His parents are taking him off to get some legal advice somewhere.'

'Well *I* felt it all right, thanks.' Ryan tugs down his collar. The bruise marks round his neck are purple from where Sharples and Zimmer grabbed him yesterday. 'Whoever it was that got Carl must've followed you both from school then to the Respect Academy,' he tells Dougie.

Dougie stares at a bus backing out. 'They must have waited. Then trailed us when we came out,' he mutters. 'Well, I didn't see them. From now on I'm gonna have eyes in the back of my head.'

'What?' I groan. 'That means they know we went to the Academy? Doyle knows? That's all I need! Flicking hell!' My stomach's going into spasms, but there's nothing to throw up there. I couldn't manage breakfast.

'Is that all you can think of!' Dougie snorts. 'Is that all you're worried about!'

'Didn't *you* see anything odd in the record shop then? Anyone you recognised?' Ryan asks him.

'Wasn't there, was I? We split. I went to Mum's office and got a lift home. Oh – and if you start spreading *this* around, Ryan,' he glares, 'you'll be in dead trouble.'

'What d'you take me for?' Ryan blinks. He stares into the distance.

'At least Doyle and Company weren't on the bus this morning,' he mutters. 'I get the heebie-jeebies when they're anywhere near – specially behind me.'

'We've got to get some practice in,' I say. 'I've got to *do* something! I can't wait for Friday and do nothing!'

'When are you gonna start thinking about the grief you've caused, instead of yourself all the time?' Dougie glares. 'They must be pissing themselves laughing at us! Really pissing themselves! Anyhow, it wouldn't have made any difference if Carl was Bruce Lee himself! Wouldn't have helped any, would it? Doyle and his lot don't play fair. What else is he planning, eh? And on Friday – who knows how many are gonna be waiting for *you*? There could be a whole crowd of them. Has that occurred to you yet?'

'Yeah! And thanks for reminding me. So what's happened to all this *Think Positive* stuff that you were all so keen on yesterday? Who was that, eh? Ryan, you and Carl, if I remember right. *Act cool. Be pro-active! Don't even think about losing! Bad attitude?*' I recite. 'Was that me? Or was that you?'

Dougie gives a lazy shrug and starts to walk away.

'Take a look at that!' Ryan blinks. 'Is that sick-making or what? Do you see what I see? Doesn't that make you want to puke? That's got to be worth three thou at least!

Phew! A Mini-Cooper S model, if I'm not mistaken. Nice respray by the looks of it. Wouldn't have gone for turquoise though. Typical poser's colour. Who's been a clever boy and passed his test then? Pass me the vomit bag, willya.'

I watch as Doyle parks in the area allotted to Sixth-Formers. Out climb Sharples, Zimmer and a tall sexy girl with long dark hair. Then a grinning Doyle gets out and leans into the car.

'He's removing the sound system,' says Ryan. 'Doesn't trust us, does he?'

12.10 Lunch break
Advice received so far:

At the Bus Stop
  'Hey, look at Pooh's eyes! Gotta watch your eyes, Pooh! Your eyes are a dead give-away – they show your fear!'
  'Yeah, I can smell it too!'
  'Yeah – that's 'cos he's wetting himself! Ha-ha-ha!'
  Sonya, Denise and Mel

On the Bus
  'Can't wait till Friday. Someone's gonna be pulped – and it's gonna be you.' Sonya, muttering into my neck, from behind
  'Where's it gonna be, then? I'm really looking forward to this! I love a good fight.' Denise

In the Car Park

'*What's all this about a fight? You aren't serious? You sure about this? Stuart Doyle? No way! Not his style, mate — especially with some nerdy Year Nine kid! Where did that come from? It's a joke, believe me, it's a joke.*' Meera's brother, Year Ten

Tutor Room, Before Registration

'*Keep calm, man, Keep calm.*' Ali Patel

'*Tell somebody. It's infantile. All you've got to do is tell someone.*' Meera

'*Look, why don't you write an anonymous letter to the Head — like it's come from someone else?*' Lauren

'*Yeah. Tell him what's going on. It's obvious. That's what I'd do. You don't have to try and be macho about it, you know.*' Jasmine (before Sonya and Mel arrived)

In Front of the Staff Pigeonholes

'*Sorry? Sorry? Sorry's not good enough, Edwin. You promised me your English book — first thing this morning! Where is it, Edwin? Where is it? Do you see your book in my pigeonhole? Do you? No! Neither do I. I want it first thing tomorrow — without fail! And a detention — we'll make it Friday, I shall be on duty then — so you'll have the pleasure of my company. You've got nothing to smile about, Edwin Tully! Nothing to smile about at all.*' Mr Day, when he collared me on the way to Double Science and covered me with spittle spray

Double Science

'*You got to stand up to bullies so they don't mess with you. They used to help themselves to my bag of Mini-Mars — just help themselves! From my briefcase! And they take the piss. Can I help it if I'm well-built for my age? I keep out of their way now, Sharples's the one I really hate. Well, give him one for me, will you? Aren't you scared?*' Nigel Pinkney, in the Science store room when we were fetching the boxes of batteries

'*Now let me get this straight. You are telling me that Stuart — Stuart Doyle has made threats against you? That something sinister is going to happen to you on Friday? At a time and designation that you don't know but are waiting to be informed of at some stage?*' (Mr Grimshaw, smiling down at me.) '*And where did this come from, might I ask? . . . Well, I'm sorry — er, — what's your name? Ed? Well, Ed, I find that quite difficult to believe. I know Stuart well — and I'm absolutely certain you've got this all wrong. Don't worry — it will amount to nothing more than a silly misunderstanding, I'm sure. We'll sort out this nonsense once and for all. First, we need to hear what Stuart has to say — if, of course, he knows anything about it all. Wait there — I'll get Mrs Cadwallader to find out where he is and send him over . . .*' Mr Grimshaw, Headmaster. Inside my head

Morning Break

'*When you need it, your adrenalin takes over. It's*

amazing what adrenalin can do. Like that woman when her kid got trapped under a car? Well, she managed to lift it off, didn't she? Adrenalin gives you strength you never knew you had.' Arun Begana

'*Hey, Ed, why don't you ring Childline? Wanna borrow my mobile?'* Mel

'*Shouldn't have got involved, mate. I'd bunk off if I was you.'* Tall spotty kid

'*Look – just say sorry. Back off. You'll only get beaten. Not worth it is it?'* . . . '*Why do boys think they have to act tough all the time?'* . . . '*We don't get it, do we?'* . . . '*No.'* The weird ginger twins

CDT

'*Have you thought of apologising to him or something? I didn't actually see what happened, but I heard about it. You were asking for it, if you want my opinion. But Stuart Doyle's OK, isn't he? Where did this stupid rumour about a fight come from, anyway? I reckon that his mates are just winding you up to teach you a lesson. All you've got to do is apologise. It's not worth it, is it?'* Andrew Paisley. Muttered under his breath, pretending to borrow my sandpaper

'*Get someone else to sneak. Get them to tell a teacher.'* Leanne Tidman. Note scrawled in rough book

By the Lockers

'*Hey, gayboy! Show us your muscles, darlin'!'*

'*Yeah! Show us your Kung Fu!'*

'*Oooooo! Respect, man! Respect!*'

Brett, Clive and Jason, putting on stupid, poofy voices. How do they know we went there? HOW DO THEY KNOW?!

∎

Five Minutes Ago, Other Side of Bushes, At Least Six Metres From the Kitchens

'*What are you doing? Urinating in the bushes! I can see you! Don't think I can't! You horrible, disgusting boys! Why can't you use the toilets, like everyone else? Get away with you before I call a teacher!*' Beady-eyed dinner lady, shouting from kitchen window at me, Dougie and Ryan

∎

Dougie's gone off in a funk. The news about Carl is going around. This time it isn't Ryan – I've been with him all morning. It was bound to get out. Loads of kids must know. Whoever did Carl over was bound to spread it around. That's the whole point!

Ryan's gone off with his little red book – he's actually got a special bet book. He's obsessed! Just an excuse, isn't it? Doesn't want to hang round with me. I spot Dougie watching Ali, Glenn and others playing footie. Andrew Paisley's in goal – useless. They keep shouting at him.

I keep getting close-ups of Doyle's face. They change. One minute, that smug, amused look, like he's laughing at you inside – only you don't get the joke. Next, that icy blue stare that scares the boxers off you. How does he do it? I can *feel* him enjoying the effect he's having. I'm so mixed up I can't remember what's real and what's rumour. I keep going over what Doyle said, trying to make some sense of it.

I prise myself from the wall. Wander over to Dougie. He acts like I'm not here. 'It isn't Ryan who's been spreading stuff about Carl,' I say. He ignores me. 'And all that stuff yesterday about a fight – fact is Doyle never even mentioned a fight.'

'Uh?' Dougie grunts, keeping his eyes on the game.

'Doyle never actually said the word *fight*.'

'So?'

'What he actually said was it would just be me and him on Friday.'

Dougie snorts. 'No way.'

'Yeah, that's what you keep telling me. But I'm telling you exactly what he *did* say. Because Ryan was the only one who heard it, and he twists things. What Doyle actually said was, "*OK – you've got four days. Enjoy them. Then we'll have a get-together – just you and me. I'll let you know where and when – put it in your diary. Then we'll see if I scare you or not.*" ' Only it doesn't sound so scary when *I* say it. It sounds totally feeble.

Dougie ignores me, keeping his eyes on Ali dribbling

the ball. Then he says, 'Stuart Doyle's not gonna stoop to some messy punch-up. It's stupid.'

'That's the point! Never said he would, did I? I don't know what's gonna happen! I'm just trying to put you in the picture. Because yesterday you bet two pound fifty on me winning a fight.'

'Yeah – must have been crazy,' Dougie mutters. 'Don't know how we let Ryan talk us into that one. If you ask me, all that is just Doyle-speak. His oily way of saying you're gonna get done. He made *that* clear in his message to Ryan. What was it? *Prepare for battle? To be knocked senseless?* I mean – who does he think he is?' he squeaks. 'The Godfather or something? He's been watching too many old films. He must really be enjoying this!' He stares ahead at the football all the time he's speaking. 'Doesn't have to be Friday. Could be today. Could be tomorrow . . . I'm gonna join Ali's game.'

His mobile bleeps. He takes it from his pocket and puts it to his ear. 'Yeah? . . . Right . . . Yeah – that'll teach 'em.' He turns his back on me and stares down at the ground. 'Is there any point? I mean . . . No— . . . I dunno— . . . When? . . . Yeah – OK . . . What? Dunno – that could get heavy— . . . Yeah – seeya.'

'That wasn't Carl, was it?' I ask.

'Yeah – as it happens,' he says fiddling with his mobile.

'What's he say?' I ask.

'I'm trying to check my messages—'

'Dougie! Tell me what he said, will you?'

'OK, OK!' he snaps. 'They've seen a solicitor. The solicitor's going to check if the shop's got video surveillance and ask to see it. It might show what happened. She told them they might be able to sue for racist remarks. But his parents don't want stuff in the papers – so they're thinking about it. And Carl's still mad, right?'

He glances down at his mobile – then frowns at it, open-mouthed. 'What? Bloody hell! I don't believe this stuff! It's sick!' He shakes his head at me and slaps the mobile into my hand. 'Here! You wanna see? Wanna see the messages I'm getting? There you go! Read them! Don't make it so obvious, willya? Hold it down! Hold it down!'

Y don't U kill yourself

'Go on – scroll down! There's more!'

I scroll down . . .

We will get U
Losers HA HA HA
U will suffer
slow and painful
kill kill kill kill kill kill
die die die die die die die

'Can't you trace them? See who's—'

'Get real! You think they're going to leave their numbers?' He snatches it back. 'I'll tell you what's gonna happen on Friday. You are gonna get done. Not by Doyle personally. He'll get some apes to do you – like they did me. The *"just you and me bit"* is where he turns up at the end and makes you grovel and beg for mercy. That'd fit the picture!'

And he marches off.

School library

I'm trying to copy some notes that Caitlin's lent me for my English homework. Why bother? First bell goes. Kids stuff books into bags. Computer screens blink and fade. Kids whose tutor base is the library start piling in. Out of the window there are figures like little ants. Clumps and strings of ants. Rippling across the tarmac into school. I can't move. What does it matter if I'm late? What does it matter?

I move out to the stairs, lean over the banister looking down the stairwell. Kids coming and kids going. Kids laughing. Second bell – swarms of kids now. Voices, footsteps echoing off the walls. Registration – I'm late. Where then? – can't remember . . .

'Is he OK?'

All these faces peering down at me.

'What happened?' says a voice.

'Must've tripped.'

'You OK, mate?'

'Maybe we ought to get a teacher.'

'No – it's OK. I'm all right.'

'You might've broken something.'

Yes, please. Please, please let there be bones broken. Hospital please. Six weeks, six months, a year even . . .

'Does it hurt anywhere?'

I get to my feet. Nothing hurts. Why doesn't it hurt?

'Here's yer bag.'

I was falling – and all the time I was thinking, *This is it, this is the answer. Thank you! Thank you! Let me break something – an arm, a leg, two legs . . . both arms and both legs! I don't mind – just get me out of Friday.* Couldn't be expected to turn up with two arms and two legs in plaster, could I?

Wouldn't think all that could go through your mind in a few seconds, would you? But it can. *Did* I trip? Did someone trip me? Dunno. All I remember is falling. Dying for a drink. Haven't had a drink all day. But then I'll be needing to pee and I'll have to chance the bogs. Not worth it. Not worth it . . .

'Oi, Ed!'

I turn to see Gareth and Ivan from 9K. 'We put three quid on you, between us,' says Ivan. 'Sixty quid if you win.'

'You'd better win,' adds Gareth.

'Yeah, no problem,' I say, all smiles like I'm believing it.

'Ryan says you've been doing martial arts for years – says you're nearly a brown belt. That true?' says Gareth.

'Shtoom,' I say tapping the side of my nose, like I don't want them spreading it about.

13.02 Afternoon registration

No Mr Hargreaves yet. Everyone lounging about.

'Ugh – look who it isn't! It's the Kung Fu Kid!' shrills Mel. She's sitting on a table, brushing Sonya's hair.

'Kung Fu woman, more like!' snorts Sonya. 'Where you been, then?' she shouts. 'Practising yer karate chops!' She acts out a slow-motion karate routine with oriental sound effects in a poncey sort of way with floppy wrists, then minces back to her table – which quite a lot of people think is hilarious.

'Hey, why didn't Carl use it, then? When he got nicked yesterday?' Mel calls. 'He could have done a Bruce Lee and sent everyone flying! Ha! Ya!' She spins round, swinging her arms and throwing kicks at invisible opponents.

Dougie's sitting with Glen and Ali, his feet up on a chair, his back to me. He doesn't even look round.

'There ain't really gonna be a fight, is there?' asks Mel. 'It's a wind-up, innit, Ryan?'

'That's for us to know and you to guess,' he blinks.

'Right everyone!' Mr Hargreaves rushes in. 'Come on, come on – back to your desks. Move it! OK, timetable change – whole school assembly straight after registration.'

A groan rumbles round the room.

'What's it gonna be about this time?' mutters Gavin Cox. 'Bogs, litter, drugs, graffiti or mobile phones?'

I flop into my seat next to Ryan. He's doodling daggers in his rough book. He turns a page and eye-signals me to look. I read: *Gareth says someone's smashed up Carl's clay footballer in the art room.*

'Now – anyone not here who should be?' Mr Hargreaves asks, opening the register.

13.10 Whole school assembly

The Deputy Head, Heads of Year and Heads of Departments are all seated at the back of the stage.

'Never guess how much money's on you,' whispers Ryan in my ear. 'One hundred and twenty-two pounds and seventy-five pence. You'd better lose, mate.'

Mr Grimshaw appears. He waits for silence, staring at someone behind us. He scans the faces in the hall. 'Here, in this school hall,' he announces, 'there are pupils who are using drugs.'

You can almost hear the swish as hundreds of heads look round, expecting to see the culprits.

'I know this for certain! Because the sad fact is that these days, there is not *one* secondary school in the country where this does not occur.' He pauses. 'I know too that some of you are dealing. Not only in hash, cannabis, dope, grass, pot – whatever you like to call it. But also in more lethal – Class A – drugs.' He points a finger. 'You know who you are! And we will find out who you are!'

Heads turn again, looking for instant confessions or give-away signs of guilt.

'An even sadder fact is that today, a boy from Year Ten was found behind the changing pavilion, throwing up from the effects of cannabis.'

Voices start to murmur round the hall. 'Quiet!' he orders. 'His so-called friends were also found in possession of drugs. Some of these were supplied in school – regrettably by someone in Year Eleven. The matter is now in the hands of the police. Their parents have been informed and all five of them have been expelled. Make no mistake!' he roars. 'Anyone found in this school in possession of drugs will be expelled. No excuses! No second chances! *Out!* I hope I've made myself clear. Good. And if anyone knows anything at all . . .'

I can see Dougie. The row in front. Sitting between Ali and Glenn. He doesn't want anything to do with me.

It won't be Doyle, will it? Maybe those pigs that got me before. How long will it take? . . .

Maybe you don't feel it when they're kicking you. Maybe I'll pass out. I wish astral projection was for real. I'd just float off like that holy man – feeling nothing . . .

What if I did grovel?

I don't know what to do. What am I gonna do? *What am I gonna do? . . .*

■

We shuffle out of the hall.

'Same old stuff,' moans Ryan. 'At least we missed a bit of History.'

I see Doyle coming out of the doors further down the corridor. He catches me looking, then looks away. Like I don't exist. Like I'm an insect turd or something. Like he's bored with me.

Suddenly I'm thinking, *What if it's not him doing all this stuff? What if it's just Sharples and Zimmer? Or Brett and his lot? Or all of them? Maybe that's what it is? Yeah. That's what it is! Just loads of kids having a go. That's how it got to be with Lester – till no one wanted to know him . . . Maybe nothing will happen on Friday. Maybe it's like Dougie said on Monday – four days of suffering. The torture of not knowing where it's going to come from next. Till I can't take any more. And I'm grovelling – begging – saying, 'Yeah – I'm scared. Stop! Please, please stop! You scare me! Please, please, just stop! I want it over!' But what if it doesn't stop? What if it goes on and on? Like it did for Lester. I can't think, can't think . . .*

'Did you hear me?'

'What?'

Ryan looks over his shoulder. 'I was saying that

Dougie's lost his bottle now,' he whispers. 'Without Carl, he's no good. He's all cool when Carl's around – different picture now though. D'you see those text messages he's getting? Sick or what?'

19.00 Home

'You sure?' asks Mum.

'Yeah – I told you! I don't mind!'

'No need to shout,' she says.

She wants to see some old film on at Cinema Déjà Vu. It's only on tonight. Ellie wants to go too, so I've offered to babysit. The instant they've gone, I'm on the phone to Ryan.

'Listen, I've got the place to myself for a couple of hours. Come round. I need to try out some of that stuff Elvira showed us. If anyone's going to do me, I'm not going to just stand there.'

'I dunno.' I hear the TV in the background.

'What d'you mean, you don't know? Come on! Look, it's better than sitting round doing nothing! You need this almost as much as I do! What's the matter? C'mon Ryan!'

'Hang on.' The phone clicks. Silence . . . Another click. 'Ed? You still there? I'm on the other phone.'

'You coming then? I've got this—'

'Look, it's doing my head in, all this. And I'd have to walk or bike down. I don't want to be caught again, do I? Sorry, mate.' And he hangs up.

I could try Carl again. I tried him when I got home – permanently engaged. I lift up the receiver. Really jittery. I feel so bad about what happened. What to do? If I don't ring, he'll think I'm not bothered. If I do, he might tell me to get lost . . . *Just do it! Just do it!*

'Hello. Sorry we cannot answer the phone. Please leave your name and message after the tone . . .'

'Hi – this is Ed for Carl. Sorry about what happened. Give us a call, will you?' My hands are sweating. I hang up.

The phone rings. I snatch it up – 'Carl?'

'No, Ed. It's me. Dad.'

'Oh – hi, Dad.

'How's it going? You all OK?'

'Yeah – I'm babysitting. Mum and Ellie have gone to the pictures.'

'So how's things with you, then Ed?'

'Yeah, fine thanks.'

'So what's new?'

'Er – Jack's got a new tooth. Oh yeah, the garage door keeps sticking – I can't get my bike out.'

'I know – your mum said. I'll fix it next time I'm down. Why don't you try some WD40? And how's school, then?'

'Well – I can't decide whether to do Art or PE for GCSE next year.'

■

I'm in Jack's room. He's fast asleep, sucking his thumb. I crouch on the toy box, listening to him breathe. His teddy bear lamp flickers – blue, red, green teddies dancing on the walls. This used to be my room. It's tiny. Feels safe in here – that talcum powder smell, his soft breathing . . .

I can see the splatter marks on the window ledge where Lester and me tried to kill this hornet with fly-spray. But we grabbed the wrong can. It was gold paint. '*Deadly to man – the hornet's sting,*' I hear Lester saying. We took turns in keeping that gold hornet. Lester reckoned it was lucky. I've got the rubber-band ball. We shared that too – it was Lester's turn next. All those rubber bands we collected. We were always on the lookout. Used to go rubber-band hunting – loads on the pavements where the posties dropped them. We rolled them together. Just this little ball at first – it grew and grew. Must have been ten – maybe twelve centimetres in diameter in the end. *Wonder if Lester's still got that hornet?* Bet he has – he never threw anything away. His room was like a junk shop . . . It wasn't really a hornet. Just a wasp.

You think you know people – but you don't. Not really. I thought I knew Lester. But I didn't, did I? I thought I knew Dougie – well maybe I did. He was always Carl's sidekick. I know Ryan, all right. But then maybe I don't. Never even liked him – but he's the only one who's still around, isn't he? Don't think I even know myself any more.

Not going to think about it! Got to get it out of my head! Stop thinking about it – nothing about Doyle . . .

That drugs thing. All over the local paper and television news. Old Grimshaw being interviewed – going on about dope, reefers, spliffs and smack, like he'd been doing homework on all the lingo. Followed by a parents' guide to druggies and the signs to look out for: dilated pupils, secretive behaviour, mood swings, excessive consumption of water etcetera etcetera.

So Mum starts giving me the third degree. Have I ever been offered stuff? Do I know anyone who has? I *would* tell her, *wouldn't* I? Then Ellie's winding me up. Saying I'm definitely on something because the first thing I did when I got home was down a whole jug of water. Also I win first prize for mood swings and furtive behaviour. Mum takes this seriously. I can feel her staring into my eyes, like she's believing I'm an ecstasy addict or something. Ellie finds this hilarious. But I don't. So I yell at them to get off my back, shut myself in my room and leave them to it. Then Mum's knocking on my door being all concerned and understanding. Going on about my hormones for flicks sake! And Ellie's shrugging and telling me, 'Look – you've got to learn to take a joke.'

I tuck the quilt over Jack. What happened to that rubber-band ball then? Must be around somewhere . . .

Here it is. In the drawer under my bed with my Subbuteo stuff. I'll measure it. Need a ruler—

What am I doing? Haven't got time for this! Got to

practise the stuff Elvira showed us. Where's that book I found in the library today? In my school bag. Here – Simple Self Defence. Some of the stuff she showed us, and more. Photos too. Got to practise. Got to practise.

I try Mum's room. Stand in front of the long mirror. Get into active stance. Good. OK, top of body facing assailant, right foot leading, hands at chest height, palms open, fingers together, right hand leading. Keep bodyweight low. Move according to how assailant moves. Knees relaxed, bent. Evade attack. Keep the right distance. Now, major body weapons. Hammer blow—

Phone's ringing again. *Ignore it. Got to practise!*

The answer-machine. 'Er, hi. Is this Ed Tully's number? It's Caitlin – never mind.' *Click.*

I run to the phone in the hall, press one four seven one, jot down the number. Stand with my hand frozen on the phone. What am I going to say?

'Hello.' I recognise her voice straight away.

'It's me. Ed.'

'Oh, hi, Ed. I looked you up in the book. Look, my mum's going to a PTA meeting – hang on . . .' I hear her calling, 'Mum – wait a minute! Hold on!' She drops the phone. I wait. 'Ed? You still there?'

'Yeah.'

'Can I come round? She can drop me off and pick me up on the way back. She's waiting for me. Look – I'm coming anyway.' *Click.*

19.25

'Did you see all that stuff on the telly?' she asks as I open the door.

'Yeah. And in the paper. Mum's convinced I'm on ecstasy just 'cos I was drinking water.'

She laughs. 'My mum read out a bit which said that kids were handing out drugs like sweets. Honestly. Like we all stand round at breaktimes pill-popping and injecting!' She follows me into the kitchen. 'That's not yours, is it?' she jokes, blinking at my old toy garage on the floor.

'Yeah. Well it was. It's Jack's now. He's Ellie's baby – Ellie's my sister. She and Mum have gone to the pictures. Wanna coffee or something?'

Can't believe she's here. Can't believe how normal I'm sounding.

'Mmm – OK.' She throws her coat on to a chair. 'I haven't been able to stop thinking about you,' she says, leaning against the fridge.

'Yeah?' I say. But it comes out sounding like, *Yeah? Hey-hey hey!*

'Not like *that*!' She's half frowning, half grinning. 'Look – why can't you be serious? Sometimes you act like everything's a big joke. What happened to Lester every day wasn't funny. Or that confrontation in the car park – even though it got a big laugh.'

'I didn't mean it like that. Look, forget it.'

'So, what's all this about a fight?' she asks. 'It *is* just a wind up, isn't it? And what's all this betting stuff? It's like Ryan is getting some sort of kick out of it! Isn't he s'posed to be your friend?' She keeps shrugging dramatically.

'Look, I don't really want to talk about it. It's my business, right?'

'Hardly. Everyone knows. Ryan's made sure of that.'

I hand her a mug of coffee. She sits down at the table. 'Well?'

It would be great to tell someone. Someone I can trust. Can I trust her? Can I?

'OK. I'll tell you exactly what Stuart Doyle said to me. But first you have to promise you won't tell anyone, right?'

'I promise.'

As I'm telling her I can read what she's thinking. Her jaw drops. She stares at me, blinking.

'That's so freaky!' she says, shaking her head. 'It's scary. What a poser! Such a big-head! He's bad loser too. That's what it's *really* about. Can't take anyone getting the better of him. Especially that you got kids laughing at him.' She leans on her elbows, chin on hands, frowning.

'What's it mean? It doesn't make sense. He won't take part in some stupid fight, though. I can't see that happening. I just can't. He's just trying to frighten you!' she announces. 'I don't think he'll actually *do* anything to you. There'd be trouble if he did and it got out. Wouldn't take the risk, would he? He gets his kicks from ridiculing people. Doesn't like it when someone does it to him, though. But with a big ego like his, he has to prove himself, doesn't he? He can't let you think you've got the better of him.'

I want to believe it. Maybe she's right. I start to tell her Dougie's theory about the four days waiting – the not knowing being all part of the punishment. Suddenly I'm remembering what they did to Dougie and Ryan and Carl. Then I'm telling her – and wishing I hadn't started. She sits there open-mouthed. 'What?' she keeps saying. 'What?'

I don't even begin on the stuff that's happened to me.

'Oh, my God,' she groans, leaning back, hugging herself.

'You mustn't tell anyone, right? No one! Promise? You have to promise.'

I shouldn't have told her. I shouldn't have told her. My inside are churning. *What if it gets out to people like Brett Paine and Sonya and that lot.* Blabbermouth. *I'm just as stupid as Ryan.*

'Yeah, OK. I promise. But it's sick. Totally sick. And you don't even know who's doing all of this?'

'No. But I know where it's coming from, don't I?'

She shrugs. 'I dunno. There are always plenty of kids who enjoy kicking people when they're down, aren't there? Who just like to put their boot in. Lower forms of life – like Sonya, Brett and that crowd.'

'Yeah. That's what makes it confusing. Sometimes I

don't know who's doing what.'

Then I try to explain Ryan's theory about the betting.

'That's so ghoulish,' she grimaces. 'Like gladiators or something. And you know, some of the girls are worse than the boys. You ought to hear some of them in the loos. And you can guess who I'm talking about. But you've got a bit of a fan club too.'

'Yeah?'

'Especially Year Seven girls.'

'Oh.'

'I'm scared,' she says. 'I thought Stuart Doyle was just a smarmy sadistic big-head. But after what you've just told me – well, he sounds like a psycho.' She frowns at me. 'Your friend Ryan,' she says, 'he's a bit odd, isn't he?'

'Is he?'

'Yeah. The way he twitches all the time.'

'He's always been like that. He's OK though,' I add. *I ought to stick up for him seeing as he's the only mate I've got at the moment.*

'What about Lester, then?' she asks.

'What about him?'

'Have you seen him?'

'No.'

'Maybe he'll tell,' she says. 'He hasn't been back to school, has he? Or perhaps he's faking being ill.'

'He's faking going to school,' I tell her. 'His mum thinks he's going to school – so he must be skiving off somewhere every day. My mum met her and she told her she's worried about Lester because he's too much of a loner.'

Caitlin leans forward, arms folded, staring down at the table. 'There was this boy in my last school. His name was Ross. He was always being picked on by this group in our class. No particular reason,' she shrugs. 'They'd refuse to let him pass unless he smiled or begged or paid them. Sometimes they'd make him say something stupid, like *Please forgive me for stinking*. He was always being pushed around, spat at, having things nicked. They even nicked his shoes during games – and he never told anyone. Not till later. It became like he was contaminated. No one would sit next to him. Kids would hold their noses and groan if he came near. Most, like me, just ignored it. But we didn't sit next to him either. I mean, you don't want to get involved, do you?

'In the end he didn't have a single friend. He was always on his own. They dangled him over a bridge once. He must have got desperate because eventually he told a teacher. She called the kids in and questioned them. They all denied it of course. The teacher told Ross to stop making a fuss and stick up for himself a bit more. Those kids jumped him on the way home and beat him up. *He lost an eye*. There was stuff about it in the newspapers.'

She looks up at me. 'You know what? His parents found a box at the top of his cupboard. Full of bottles of deodorants and sprays. Like he really believed he stank. And I could picture him – trying desperately, showering and spraying himself, thinking it would make a difference, and—'

She leaps up and snatches a paper towel from the roll on the worktop. 'Sorry,' she says. 'Sorry.' She blows her nose. Her eyes are watery. 'It just makes me so angry. With myself too. Because none of us did anything. They wouldn't have got away with it if we'd *all* said something. He was this really nice kid! And they totally destroyed him. It was all a game to them. *Just having a laugh*, that's what they said.' She's picking the paper towel to shreds.

'That sounds like Lester,' I tell her.

'Anyway, that's why I think you should tell someone.'

'I can't.'

'You can! Look, I'll back you up. What about your mates? I'll find some others—'

I shake my head. 'Don't think I haven't thought about it. But it won't work.'

'Yes it would—'

'No! It won't! For starters, it's my word against his! And it sounds so stupid. Anyway, nothing's actually happened to *me*, has it? Well, nothing that anyone could pin on him personally. And for seconds, Doyle and his mates could just laugh it off – say that what he said was a joke. Only me and Ryan heard it, anyway. Can you imagine what sort of life I'd have if I grassed and no one believed me? If they didn't take it seriously? Like the story you just told me. Can you imagine that? I can! And I'd rather just get a good kicking and have it over and done with, than everlasting torture like that boy Ross.'

She sits with her head in her hands, staring down at her cold coffee.

'But thanks, anyway,' I shrug. 'Look – it's Thursday tomorrow. Only one more day – then it'll all be over. A bit like going to the dentist.' I can't believe I'm saying these things.

'It's nothing like—'

She's interrupted by a loud wailing noise.

'What's that?' she stares.

■

'Meet Jack. He's teething. Can you pass me that tube there – on the mantelpiece.'

We sit on the sofa. I rub some teething gel on to Jack's gums. Caitlin sits grinning at me.

'Wow, you really look as if you know what you're doing.'

'You haven't seen anything yet. Champion bum-wiper, nappy-changer, burper – can you turn that light off? Thanks.'

'Ah, look – he's nodding off,' she whispers.

She's got this soft gooey look. And it makes me feel a bit gooey too.

'You're scared, aren't you?' she says.

'Yeah. Yeah – I am.'

I shouldn't have said that. Now I'm reminded *how* scared I am. And I don't want her to see it.

'I'll be lying in bed worrying about you,' she says.

'Yeah? Well, I'll be lying in bed worrying about me, too.'

'See? You're doing it again. Why can't you be serious?'

I carry Jack back to his cot.

'What's this?' she asks when I get back. She holds up my rubber-band ball. So I tell her.

'How long were you friends with Lester, then?'

'Ages – from when we were about five or something.'

'D'you miss him?'

'Yeah – sometimes.' *Why am I telling her this stuff?*

'What's he like?'

'Mad. Crazy. Had this weird sense of humour—'

'What's the matter?' she asks.

'Just realised. I said he *had*, not *has*. He doesn't have much to laugh about these days, does he?'

'He always looks a bit—' she shrugs.

'What?'

'Feeble, I s'pose.'

'Feeble? Nah. He was never feeble. He was full of ideas – odd stuff. Totally bonkers sometimes. Like he lived in his own world. Never knew what he was going to come up with next. He'd invent these amazing stunts and games. He could be really funny. Off-the-wall funny. I mean, the stuff he did! His mum didn't have a clue.'

'Like what?'

'What? No, you'd think it was just stupid. Girls don't have the same sense of humour.'

'You mean, like jokes about bums, willies, boobs, farting and stuff?'

'No!' I'm laughing. I'm actually laughing. 'OK. I'll tell you a true story. Not sure I should, though. I've never told anyone this. My mum would do her nut if she knew about it. So would his.'

'You've got to tell me, now,' she says. 'Or I'll die of suspense.'

'Well, one school holiday – we were about eleven or twelve . . . yeah, that's right. Easter holidays, it was. I get this phone call from Lester. "*Is your mum or anyone in?*" he asks. So I say, "*No, why?*" And he says, "*Wait there!*"

'So I'm waiting, when I hear a car horn hoot. I look out of the window and see Lester's mum's car on the drive. But I can't see Lester, just his mum in the driving seat. So I go out, but it's not his mum. It's this girl. Quite good-looking, long blonde hair. Like it could be Lester's older sister. Except he hasn't got an older sister. And she says, "*Want to go for a ride then, Ed?*"

'And I'm staring at her, thinking, *Where's Lester? What's going on?* And this girl is grinning at me – then starts laughing. And then I realise. It is Lester!'

'Lester!' shrieks Caitlin.

'Yeah. He's borrowed his mum's clothes and a blonde wig from somewhere. I dunno – his mum's probably. She's like that – very good-looking. Could be a model. Anyway, as calm as you like, he says, "*You coming or not?*" So I get in – and he says, "*Fasten your seat-belt, then.*" '

'How did he learn to drive?' says Caitlin.

'His mum had given him a few goes. She's a driving instructor – got her own driving school out by the airport. It's got a big off-road car park where he could practise. Anyway, off we went—'

'A joy ride?' says Caitlin.

'Joy ride? You're joking. It was like taking a trip with your gran. I was saying, "*Come on! Can't you go a bit faster?*" "*No,*" he says. "*I'm a very careful driver. Stop fidgeting – I'm trying to concentrate.*" '

Caitlin hoots with laughter.

'Turns out that it's not the first time he's borrowed the car. He's done a few practice runs on his own. He was quite tall, even then. I mean, he fooled me. He could get away with it. So we go on this little tour – tootling round some housing estate, where he shows off his three point turns. Then we drive back to his house. He parks it in the garage, changes back to his own stuff and by the time his mum's back, we're playing Subbuteo.'

Caitlin's frowning at me. 'Did he like dressing up in girls' clothes, then?'

'What? No – I dunno! Only for driving, I think. He

wouldn't have got away with it in his own stuff, would he? He looked at least eighteen in his mum's gear. Look, I know it sounds strange – but it was the sort of thing he did. I didn't even give it much thought at the time. It was just fun – and funny. We did it quite a few times. No one had a clue.'

'He sounds brilliant,' she grins. Then she looks serious. 'It makes it worse. I've never seen him like that. It's hard to imagine. Only seen him like, well you know, as victim. Like that boy, Ross.' She lets out a big sigh. 'D'you think Lester might tell his parents? About all the bullying I mean. If he told – it would all come out. There'd be big trouble. You'd be all right, then.'

'Oh yeah? Make it worse, more like. And, it's too late now, isn't it? It's been going on for ages. He's just put up with it. Anyway, it's only him and his mum. He didn't have a dad. Well, not that he ever mentioned. And Lester probably wouldn't want to worry his mum.'

'You ought to be proud that you stuck up for him like that,' she says. 'I am. Even though it was crazy.'

She looks at me. And I look at her. And I can't think of anything to say. I get this weird dreamy tingling feeling and – the doorbell rings.

'That'll be my mum,' she blinks . . .

Just as Caitlin reaches the car, I remember. 'Hold on! I've still got your rough book.'

She follows me back in and I fetch my school bag. 'It's down the bottom – hang on a sec.'

I tip it out on to the carpet. 'Here it is. Thanks . . . See you tomorrow, then.'

She's looking at me like she's going to say something. But then she just smiles and leaves.

■

I lie on the sofa, turning the ball over in my hand, staring at it. Yeah. I do miss Lester. There's no one like him. Does he miss me? Thought he might have called me after Monday. Thought he might say, '*Thanks, mate.*' Why didn't he? All it takes is a phone call. Maybe he's thinking the same thing? Maybe he knows what I'm going through – doesn't want to complicate things. Maybe he's waiting for me to—

This is stupid, this is! I'm gonna call him! Should have done it ages ago. After The Wall of Death. Both of us waiting for the other one. It's stupid!

I leap up. Why didn't I do this before? Suddenly, nothing seems so urgent, so important, so obvious. I'm gonna call him! I'll tell him what's been happening. I'll say, '*Hey Lester – it's me.*' No. I'll say, '*Ishka-boodle!*' And he'll answer, '*Zom koo-rah!*' Then together we'll chant, '*Ishka-ishka-boo! Ra! Ra! Ra!*'

Know his number off by heart, don't I? My heart's going like the clappers . . .

'Hello?' A man's voice.

'Can I speak to Lester, please?'

'Sorry, you've got the wrong number.'

'What? Is this six, nine, three, double six, nine?'

'Yes.'

'Is there a Mrs Carroll – Mrs Tina Carroll – there?'

'No. You've definitely got the wrong number.'

'Wait. How long have you had that number?'

'Over a year now.'

'You don't have a number or address for Mrs Carroll, then.'

'Sorry, no.'

I grab the phone book – there are seventeen Carrolls listed for round here. I try them all – no luck. *Where have they moved to then?* I feel down now. Frustrated. Need to talk to Lester. Where is he?

My school books and stuff are all over the floor. Mum'll be home soon. She'll start going on. I haven't done my homework. *Toss homework!*

I'm staring down at a white envelope. Half-sticking out of my Maths book. A small one this time.

For the Attention of Edwin Tully

How'd it get there? Made sure today. Kept my bag where I could see it, all the time. The stairs – when I tripped on the stairs. *Here's yer bag.* Didn't trip, did I? I was tripped . . .

Phone's ringing again. Let it ring. Answer-machine clicking on.

'Ed. It's me again.'

I heave myself up and go to the phone. 'Hi.'

'You OK?' asks Caitlin.

'Yeah.'

'Just thought I'd let you know about the PTA meeting. It was mostly about that drugs thing. Mum's been going on about it all the way home, especially about one of the parents there. He got really bolshy with another parent. This woman was trying to say that making soft drugs like cannabis sound as dangerous as cocaine was misleading. That kids being fully informed was important in drugs education – and so on. Anyway, this other parent, a man, he got really pushy. A real know-it-all, Mum said. Tried to make the woman look a total twat. There was quite a row, with people taking sides – though the drugs officer who was there backed up what the woman was saying. But, guess who the man was? Someone called Anthony Doyle. Sound familiar? Yeah – Stuart Doyle's father! He's one of the school governors, by the way.'

22.05 My bedroom

For the attention of Edwin Tully

Open it – or not? Something inside. Lumpy. *Go on. You got to open it. No choice*.

A little parcel of folded paper inside. *Do I really want to see this?*

Unfold it. A message in red ink.

You're gonna die. Why don't you just kill yourself instead of being mushed into a pulp?

Sellotaped underneath – a razor blade.

■

Other Helpful Advice Received:

'*Don't turn up.*' Leanne

'*Learn hypnotism. Put him in a trance and tell him to take a walk on the railway line.*' Paul Young

'*I wouldn't get out of bed if I was you.*' Frizzy-haired fat boy in library

'*Grow up – stop acting like someone you're not. Why don't you just tell someone?*' Jasmine

■

What am I going to do?

Don't push the panic button yet. Lester, Year Four, when I got my tongue caught in the zipper of my Dennis The Menace pencil case.

Don't push the panic button yet.

Don't push the panic button yet.

Don't push the panic button yet.

Don't push the panic button yet . . .

I need some music to take my mind off things. Stupid. My CD-player got nicked, didn't it?

01.23

Full moon tonight – feels like I'm not here.

How does Lester put up with it? Not four days. Hundreds of days.

Look – I climbed The Wall of Death didn't I? I was terrified. But I climbed it. If I could do that – I can get through this.

Which is worse? Knowing what's gonna happen? Or not knowing?

At least I've bluffed it. No one knows how scared I am. Do they?

This is useless. If I try to stay *awake* – that sometimes works. Stare at something. No blinking. You mustn't close your eyes, you mustn't close your eyes, you mustn't . . .

Uncle Edwin's staring at me from the wall. Dad had his old photo enlarged into a poster for me. Weird calling him Great Uncle Edwin – he was only fifteen in that photo. Taken when he signed up in 1914. Wearing his new uniform. Smiling, pleased with himself. Lied about his age. Couldn't have fooled anyone. Looks younger than me. He and his mates all enlisted on the same day. Eleven of them.

Edwin John Tully. Dad's hero – who I'm named after. When I was a kid and getting fed up with all that *Pooh* joking and I was moaning about my name, Dad sat me down. He told me I ought to be proud. Told me a little bit about Edwin. Said one day, when I was old enough, he'd let me read his war diaries and letters. Dad's got all his stuff. Well, what there was of it. Some letters to his mum from the trenches and a few of his diaries. One of his mates brought those home and gave them to his mum.

OK, Edwin. What would you do?

Look after your feet, mate. Keep them dry . . . And don't stick your head above the parapet.

Too late. Any other tips?

It's the waiting that's the worst. That's what gets to you. Sometimes sitting for hours in the trenches doing nothing is harder than going over the top.

I remember that bit. Like I can hear his voice inside my head. Read that in one of his diaries. Dad let me read some – not all of them. Says I've got to wait till I'm older. So there must be some terrible stuff in them. What he let me read was bad enough.

16 December 1916

Went over the top today. Sid Sykes who was right next to me got his head blown off. What's left of him is still in the trench, just a few feet away from where I'm sitting. Pissing down as usual. He's bloody lucky – at least it was over quick. Poor Georgie Owen got shrapnel in the chest. Took him hours to die. Out of the ten lads that enlisted with me, I'm the only one left.

I've stuck some cloth in my ears so I can't hear the voices. The wounded beggars still out there in No Man's Land, pleading for help. Some poor sod was begging for someone to shoot him and put him out of his misery. I hope that when my number comes up it's all over quick. It's been raining for five days now and my feet are starting to rot. What I'd give to be warm, clean and dry.

Dad's got some of his letters, too. The ones Edwin wrote home.

3 March 1917
Dear Mum, Flo, Hilda, Ivy, Nellie, Ethel, Dora and Maudie,

Thanks for the socks, Mum. Have you sent other parcels? Haven't had any for weeks now. Could do with some fags and chocolate. Has Hilda had her baby yet?

We spend a lot of time sitting on our arses – sorry Mum, posteriors. So it gives me lots of time for thinking.

We're hoping for some leave before long. So Ivy, how about making me one of your steak-and-kidney puddings? Sometimes, I dream of those – lovely soft meat and gravy. Just the ticket. We sit around talking about all the food we're going to eat when we get back – it doesn't half get the juices going.

I'm looking forward to seeing you all. I can't tell you how much. I imagine myself walking down the lane and seeing you all waiting for me. The fire blazing in the grate and all of us round the table with Mum telling me not to gobble my food – this war all finished and done with. Not too long now, eh? They tell us it'll all be over and done with by Christmas.

Keep the parcels coming.
Love Eddie

Dad took me to France last year, to see the war graves. Thousands of them, row on row on row. Boys, men, old men. And long lists of names of those whose bodies were never found.

We found Edwin's grave. He didn't make it home. Got killed two days before Christmas 1917, aged eighteen. Three of those years in the trenches. Received a medal afterwards and a citation: *For conspicuous courage in the face of the enemy, in retrieving five wounded men when under direct fire, being the last able man at his post.*

Didn't even get to be a man, did he? Just one year, seven months older than me when he had that photo taken.

If Edwin could do all that – spend three years in the trenches – what about me? Four days – that's all it is. Four days and maybe a doing over. What's that compared to what he went through? If he could do all that, then so can I. I'm gonna be like Edwin. I'm going to think about when it's all over. When I can live a normal life.

I line them up along the top of a trench: Doyle, Sharples, Zimmer, Brett, Clive, Jason, Sonya, Denise, Mel and all the others who think Lester and me are jokes – who made Lester's life a misery.

I aim my machine gun and I start firing. First at Doyle, then the rest. I watch the fear in their faces as I fire and they topple screaming into the trench.

THURSDAY

10.20 English

I'm keeping my head down. *Yes, Mr Day. No, Mr Day.* Trying to look like I'm working. Joke is I got a B plus for that *Merchant of Venice* homework – thanks to Caitlin's notes. I'm trying to give her a wide berth. I'm trying not to catch her eye. Don't want to contaminate her. That's what it feels like – as if I've got some sort of infectious disease. I keep feeling her looking at me.

No sign of Doyle today. Zimmer and Sharples are back on the bus again. Still no Carl, and no Dougie either. He must have skived off. He's been going out of his way to avoid me, anyhow. Ryan says that Dougie had been muttering about Seth – another cousin. A real hard man, he says. I've heard Carl mention him before, he's been in prison for something. But Dougie was saying that if anyone else tries anything again on him or Carl, Seth will know about it and they won't know what's hit them. Well, that's Ryan's version anyway. Ryan was getting really excited about it – going into details of what they could do to Zimmer, Sharples and Doyle. He really hates them – especially Zimmer and Sharples. Says he'd love to see them getting it –

how he'd watch and laugh. I'd watch and laugh too. Yeah – I would.

12.35 School library

Out of the window I can see Caitlin down below, walking round, arm in arm with friends. I understand now why Lester spent so much time in here – it's the only place where they leave you alone. I'm fed up with kids ignoring or pestering me – all that gloating, nudging and whispering. And in Maths, Denise turning round and making a face like I had a bad smell. I had to put up with all her hair-flinging as usual.

There's Ryan. Mooching about. He looks a bit lost. Wandering over to where Ali and others are kicking a ball about. Walking off now. Looking around like he's searching. Looking up. Too late – he's seen me.

■

'So this is where you hide out.'

He drops into the chair next to me. 'Guess what?' he says.

'Look Ryan,' I whisper. 'I don't wanna know how many bets – or how much money you've taken, OK? I'm sick of it – it's not a game.'

'Don't have to tell *me*,' he mutters. He starts fidgeting with the keys on the computer keyboard in front of him.

'Just leave it, Ryan!'

He sighs, slides down into the chair, stares out of the window, chewing his nails. 'You know that bloke, Houdini,' he says.

'Keep your voice down, will you?'

Ryan leans up close. 'I got a book about him – and there was this thing on telly about him too. He was such a wicked escape artist, see—'

'You get me, Ryan, you really do. Are you gonna lend me your book, so I can learn to be an escape artist? What a pity you didn't think of that before. Carl would have found that handy, wouldn't he? And Dougie – in the bogs. And me too. Could've flushed myself down the pan.' I feel like shouting at him, but all I can do is whisper. It'd be funny if it wasn't so tragic.

He leans forward, head in his hands. 'Wish *I* could escape,' he blinks. 'I'm scared – honest.'

'*You?* It's *me* that ought to be scared. And I'm not scared – I'm terrified!'

He chews at his thumbnail – spits it out. His nails are bitten right down. And I start feeling sorry for him: *What am I doing? Why am I feeling sorry for him?* Then suddenly I'm hating him – for making me feel sorry for him.

He stares out of the window. 'Houdini did the most amazing stuff,' he goes on. 'Handcuffed in a chained box underwater – loads of things like that. He'd invite anyone to punch him in the gut, as hard as they could. He'd trained himself see? Could control his stomach muscles, so they were rock hard. But he was just this little guy. Some people thought he had magic powers. But it was all about training – and preparation.'

'Yeah, Ryan. But he died, didn't he? When someone punched him in the stomach too hard – ruptured his spleen or something. I saw that programme too.'

'Yeah, but only because he had a dodgy appendix. And then this guy tricked him – punched him when he wasn't ready. I've been training my stomach muscles. What I do is . . .'

He mumbles on and on. I pick up my bag and leave him there. Need some peace. Don't want to talk about stupid Houdini. Don't want to think about it. Want to think about something else – anything. I snatch a book from the shelf, open it . . .

The surface temperature of the sun is six thousand degrees centigrade. This can rise to at least fourteen million degrees near the core. Within its globe, nuclear transformation takes place. Its energy keeps the sun shining. Never look at the sun directly – or through a telescope or binoculars – it could result in permanent blindness . . . The sun has enough fuel to burn for another five thousand million years . . .

First bell starts to ring . . . Think about the sun – *enough fuel to burn for five thousand million years, five thousand million years – never look at the sun – never look at the sun . . .*

'Zimmer gave me this, to give to you. Don't ask me what it is – he didn't tell me, though I've got a good idea. Told me to say they'll be in touch.' Ryan shoves a small parcel at me, shrugs and slouches off.

Somewhere to open it? That corner. It's Sellotaped – won't come off. What is it? what is it? . . .

A mobile phone? *Why have they sent me a mobile?* Dummy. You know why.

13.10 Games – the changing rooms

'Oi! Edwina!' Clive's voice.

'Just wait there a minute, darlin'!' sniggers Brett. 'Wanna take a good look at you – while you're still in one piece!' Pretending to take a photo.

'She's dead ugly, ain't she?'

Ignore them, ignore them . . .

Ryan – looking panicky – darts off and squeezes himself into a gap on the bench between Dougie and Ali.

'Right you lot! Quiet!' Mr Jones stands there. 'Someone to fetch the footballs from the store.'

Ryan's first to volunteer. He goes off with Paul. I dump my bag on an empty bench.

'Ooooo – take a look at *her*!' Jason minces up and down. 'Get out Edwina! You don't belong 'ere! Go on – go and join the women!'

Hoots and laughs echo back at me.

There's a whole lot more – but I'm not listening. Not listening. Not listening. I look down at the floor. Don't look up – *the surface of the sun is six thousand degrees centigrade – the surface of the sun—*

'Poofter!'

Brett's boots right in front of me. Don't look up – *never look directly at the sun—*

'Fairy!'

. . . or through a telescope or binoculars—

'Wee Willie Winnie!'

. . . it could result in permanent blindness—

'Hasn't got a willie has she?'

The sun has enough fuel to—

'Oi! Winnie! Winnie Wanker!'

'Haven't you, Winnie Wanker? Haven't you got a willie? Can't wank without a willie, Winnie!'

'Show us Winnie! Show us yer willie! We'll leave you alone then.'

. . . to burn for five thousand million years—

'Don't be shy, Winnie! C'mon! Let's have a look!'

Hands grabbing me. Brett's arms around my neck.

'Get off! Leave me, willya! Get flicking off!'

Tugging at my trousers – at my pants – struggling. Bastards! Bastards!

'Aaaagh!'

Got Brett! I got him! Got him! Got him on the floor! Got him in an arm lock! Gonna break his arm! I am! Gonna make him scream . . .

Agh! Someone pulling my head back – being kicked – pulled off . . .

'You've had it now, you faggot!'

Ooof!

'Yeah – that's right! Kick him in the kidneys!'

'And one from me!'

'You're gonna pay for that, you poofing wanker!'

Dragging me, dragging me – the showers – Brett grinning down at me – the smell of warm piss as it splatters over my head . . .

■

'You all right?'

Ryan crouched down in his football kit. Scared white face, blinking at me.

'Ed? Mr Jones wants to know where you are.'

'Never look at directly at the sun—'

'Do what?'

'Or through a telescope or binoculars—'

'Look, Ed – if you don't come out soon he's gonna want to know why.'

I drag myself up and turn on the shower. *Water. Clean, clean water.*

'Ed, are you OK? Does it hurt? Hold on . . . Look – here's yer towel.'

Within its globe nuclear transformation takes place—

'I've got something to show you, Ed.'

Its energy keeps the sun shining—

'Look, Ed . . .'

Through the steam I see Ryan – holding a couple of rounders bats.

'Nicked 'em from the store.' He swings one above his head. Brings it crashing down on to an imaginary enemy. 'Surprise is your biggest weapon. Remember?' He holds one out to me. 'I'll tell him you're on yer way, then shall I? Want me to shove it in yer bag? Bloody hell! Say something, Ed. Say something, willya!'

Never look directly at the sun . . .

15.20 Central Library

One of Uncle Edwin's mates shot himself in the foot when he couldn't take any more. Dad said lots of soldiers tried that. Some went loony and wandered off. Shell-shock it was. They were brought back and shot for desertion.

What if *I* had an accident – a bad accident? What if I fell down some stairs – walked in front of a car? Don't wanna *die* – just want to escape . . .

Wish I could go home. Too early – Ellie could be there, she doesn't have college on Thursday afternoons. Can't risk it. Can't risk it. Can't think where else to go – give it another ten minutes. I usually get home about quarter past. Yeah – I'll leave in ten minutes. It'll be over tomorrow – everything back to normal. Who are you kidding? Just want it over – just want it over – just want it over—

A mobile is ringing – annoying tune. A woman looks up staring at me. It's coming from my bag. Forgot, didn't I – forgot about the mobile . . .

'Excuse me. Didn't you see the sign? Mobiles switched off in the library, thank you.'

Library foyer

'Hello, Edwin.' Doyle's voice.

'We seem to have got cut off there. Hope you've recovered from that nasty business in the cloakrooms. How d'you like the phone, then?'

'What d'you want?'

'A little chat, that's all . . . Edwin? You aren't going to go all silent on me, are you? Well, let's assume you're still listening, even if you're not talking. Now, how would you like me to let you off?'

'What?'

'I'm offering you a way out.'

'What? What d'you mean?'

'Don't sound so worried, Edwin. It's a game. Everything's a game.'

'But I—'

'Wait for instructions, Edwin. Watch the messages, Edwin. Turn it off now, Edwin, there's a good boy. Check every half hour and follow instructions.'

'Look—'

He's cut me off.

16.40 Home

Can't find my key – must have fallen out of my pocket in the changing rooms. No, s'all right – s'all right – got it . . .

The door opens before I get the key in.

'Ed – what the hell is going on?' Ellie stands in the doorway, with Jack in her arms. 'Right. You are going to tell me everything, Ed. Everything!'

■

'I want to know what's going on at school, Ed.'

Ellie is sitting on the arm of the sofa. Jack is trying to climb on to my lap. I can't believe it's the same day, the same world.

'Well, Ed?'

'What are you going on about?'

'You know what! Josie and Andrea have been telling me all about it. I do still have friends at school, remember? They told me what you said to Stuart Doyle. That was stupid! Really stupid! Josie said it got a big laugh – thought it was pretty funny herself. So do I, actually. But I can't believe he'll let it go. I mean, what possessed you to do it? He's not someone to make a joke of. That was really dumb, Ed!'

'If you know so much, why ask me?'

'They told me there's talk of a fight?'

I shrug and make a *how-should-I-know?* face.

'Come on, Ed. Andrea said that you made him look like a right jerk in front of everyone! That he marched back and said something to you. So what did he say?'

'I dunno. Muttered "*Be careful*", or something. That he could be really scary if he wanted. Can't remember exactly.'

'Look, I *know* Stuart. And he *can* be truly scary.' She stares at me. 'So where does all this talk about a fight come from, then?'

'He didn't even mention the word! That's Ryan that is! Inventing stuff – spreading it around.'

'Ah, yeah – Ryan. He's the one that's going round taking bets, right? Bets on the fight that isn't going to happen? Come on, Ed!'

'I can't tell you what I don't know, can I? Sounds to me like you know more than I do!' I get up and head for the door.

'If anything happens, if there's any bother, you tell me – pronto! Right?' she calls after me.

'OK!'

She follows me out, calling up as I climb the stairs.

'I'm not joking, Ed! There's stuff you don't know about Stuart!'

I look down at her. 'Like what?'

'I know what he's like, Ed. I've known him for ages. He gets bored easily. Likes playing games and taking risks. Thing is some people only see one side of Stuart. But if you get on the wrong side of him – watch out! He manages to get away with things because he knows how to switch on the charm when he wants. Or by, I dunno – blackmail. I wouldn't be a bit surprised. Mr Fletcher, our last Chemistry teacher – you could see he was scared of him. Stuart used to make him look like a total geek in lessons. He only lasted two terms. I've seen Stuart make some people's lives a misery. He's a control freak, Ed. I'm telling you for a reason. If there's any trouble – you tell me, right? You wouldn't believe what he gets away with.'

'Right! So you'd give him a warning would you? That'd scare him off, that would.'

'It's not a joke, Ed.'

17.00 My bedroom
No message. Did I want a message? Yeah – a message saying GAME OVER.

17.30
Still no message.

18.00

> *Pale and weary*
> *the boy noble looks afraid*
> *Will he prove himself?*
> *The game unfolds*
> *The fates await*
> *U and me boy noble*

1830 at the dog walk
Baxter Place
behind old greenhouse
How will it end?

What's it mean? What's it about? I know what it is! It's fantasy role-play stuff. Like Warhammer, isn't it? Like I'm a character in a game. How does he know I played that stuff? Me and Lester were mad about it – used to play it in the Juniors at after-school club. Is he really giving me a way out? Or is it all part of the game? Don't trust him. But if it's a way out, though? . . . Got to go. Ought to go now or it'll be too late. Dark outside. Tipping down—

What?

I don't believe it! I don't believe it! There's Lester! Walking down the road! It *is* him, isn't it? Yeah – it's him! It's him! It's Lester! After all this time! I've never been so pleased to see anyone! He's seen me! He's seen me! He's at the gate! It's definitely him! He's waving – a slow arc with both hands. And I'm grinning, waving back.

'WAIT! WAIT!' I shout. I tug my shoes on, rush down the stairs, grab my coat from the hall . . .

'Hold on – hold on! Where you going?' Mum's calling after me.

The door slams behind me. Where is he? Where's Lester? He's gone. He can't have! He's here somewhere!

Must be. I run up the road. Where is he? Did something scare him off? Is this something to do with Doyle? What's going on?

18.25 The dog walk

Where did Lester get to? Is he here, ahead of me? Is this one of Doyle's tricks? Part of the game? Lester was *there* – at the gate! So what made him take off like that? Doesn't make sense – doesn't make sense. He's a lure! Doyle's using him as a lure – to get me here!

It's pissing down. I'm soaked. And it's dark – only a couple of feeble lampposts. No one about. Is that someone? Or just a shadow? Can't see – can't see! Surrounded by trees and bushes. I could be murdered here – no one would know. Where *is* Doyle? Is this the game? He'll have Zimmer and Sharples with him! They're gonna jump me, aren't they? I'm mad! What did I come here for? Got to get away! Get away . . .

'Welcome Edwin, boy noble.' Doyle's voice.

I spin round. No one there.

'Fate marks you out. You have a destiny. A mission.'

He's laughing at me. I can just make him out now – under that big tree. Can't see his face clearly – too dark. Is he on his own? I can't see anyone else. 'What've you done with Lester?'

'I'm not interested in Lester, boy noble. I have a task for you. The prize will be worth the journey.'

'I'm not gonna play your stupid games!'

'You're playing it now, Edwin. You've been playing it since Monday.'

'Where's Lester?'

A torch flashes on. I can't see anything but glare.

'You're a puzzle, you know that? What shall I do with you, Edwin? What are my options? Let's see. Make sure you get a good pummelling? Teach you the lesson you deserve? Mmm – maybe . . . Forgive and forget? Sorry, can't do that . . . Or find an alternative arrangement? Shame it's got to end, really. Haven't had so much fun in ages.'

'You sent Lester round to my house, didn't you?'

The torch goes out and suddenly he's standing right in front of me. He's laughing, 'You get me – you really do,' he says. 'Still worrying about poor old Lester, are we? I like that. Loyalty. That sort of loyalty, it's something quite rare. You know that?'

He's done something to Lester. What's he done? 'You don't give a toss about anyone! You're sick!' I shout. I don't care any more. If he's gonna do me, he's gonna do me! I'm not gonna whimper and beg for mercy. Not going to give him the satisfaction.

'You think I hate you, don't you?' he says. 'You've got it wrong. It's nothing *personal*. But you must see that you have to pay for what you did. You know something, Edwin? It's been very entertaining, guessing what you were going to do next. Me, Tony and Christos have had quite a few bets on you. Naturally, I'm in the lead – but then I've helped things along a bit . . . All that sweaty desperation to become fighting machines! But where are your friends now, Edwin? The trouble is you've become so predictable. It's getting boring. That little display of fighting spirit today was quite something, though. Not that *I* had anything to do with that one – but I'm kept informed. Now, I think we need to pep it up a bit. So, which way are you going to go, Edwin? Which way will you choose? It's important. I've got quite a lot resting on you at the moment.'

'You're *sick*!'

'You're repeating yourself, Edwin. You know, it's been quite tricky deciding what to do with you. You deserve some punishment for getting a laugh at my expense. But the fact is I've grown quite fond of you. So, I'm being generous – here's a little challenge for you. If you succeed – you go free.'

'And if I don't?'

'Well – tomorrow's Friday. We'll have to have our meeting and decide, won't we? All will be revealed. Believe me, you'd be sensible to take the offer. If I win, then you win – so we both win.'

'What do I have to do?'

'Very very simple, Edwin. Come here.'

I don't trust him—

'Don't worry. I'm not going to hurt you. Here—'

He's holding something.

'All you have to do is deliver it. There'll be someone

waiting – flat 6A, Sidney House, Palace Road. They'll give you something, you'll give it to me. Don't let me down, boy noble. I'll be in touch. Wait for instructions.'

He hands me a Smarties tube. I shake it. It's definitely not Smarties inside.

'It's drugs, isn't it? It's drugs! I don't wanna have anything to do with it!'

'You have to make a choice, Edwin. Make the right choice and you'll be free. Wait for instructions, Edwin.' He walks away.

Look at me – I'm shaking. I'm shaking.

19.30 My bedroom
No message.

Palace Road – not far from here. I could nip out – be there and back in twenty-five, thirty minutes at the most. No one'd know. Then I'd be free wouldn't I? It'd be over. But it's drugs – I'm sure it's drugs. Could be heroin, could be cocaine! What if it's a set-up? What if I got caught? I could say I was made to do it! Could be my one chance to finish it. I'm gonna do it. If I don't, someone else will. Makes no difference in the long run. It's not like I'm a real drugs runner, is it? I'm gonna do it. I'll wait till eight, then I'll do it. It's the only way out.

20.00
No message.

Right – that's it! I'm going! *But what if it's a trap?*

What if he blackmails you into doing it again? Then again? He might never let you off. Never.

Phone rings.

'Ed – for you!' Mum calls.

Is it Doyle? Why doesn't he use the mobile? I go to Mum's room, pick up the phone.

'Yeah?'

'It's me – Ryan.' His voice is croaky. Shaky.

'Ryan?'

'You delivered it yet?'

'What? What're you talking about?'

'You know what. He's made me ring you to find out.' He keeps sniffing, like he's crying.

'What? You know about it, then? Are you part of this?'

'Made *me* deliver something, didn't he? To someone in Budgen's car park.'

'When?'

'Just now.'

'What? You've done it?'

'Didn't give me no choice, did he?' He sounds terrified. 'And I've got this packet under me bed. I think it's money, Ed. It's doin' my head in, this – it's really doin' me head in. You better do it, Ed. This is all your fault! He'll do us both if you don't. You've gotta ring him when you've done it. You've got till half nine. If you haven't phoned by then it'll mean you haven't delivered. So you make certain you do it – or we're both for it! You got to use this number. Ready?'

20.20

Lying on my bed, staring at the ceiling. Wishing I could astrally project myself – anywhere but here. Wish I'd paid attention to how to do it. Still wearing my coat. Got to the door and bottled out. He's using me as a runner. That's how it happens. It won't be the only time, will it? If I do it, he'll blackmail me into doing it again and again and again.

Thing is, I haven't been thinking properly. Mustn't panic. I've got to think. This is a game. And I'm a player in the game, that's what he said. '*I've helped things along a bit.*' And he's the game master. *He* controls the game. '*Which way are you going to go, Edwin?*' He's gambling with Zimmer and Sharples on what I do. Whether I go one way or the other. If he's right about what I do next, he'll win. If *he* wins, so do I. And he'll let me off. That's what he said. So what's he thinking I'm going to do? Think! Think!

I jump up, walk up and down. I don't know! If I don't know, how can he? It's like he thinks he knows me better than I do myself!

Stuff him. I'm not going to play his games! I'm not doing it! I'm not going to be his errand boy! Is that what he's expecting me to think? What's the right decision?

No choice is there? That's what Ryan said. No choice. Yeah – there is! There *is* a choice. '*You choose, Edwin.*' Was that a clue? Was it? He's gambling on the choice *I*

make – on what he knows about *me*. '*You choose, Edwin*.'
Yeah. *I* choose. *I* choose. I choose *not* to do what Stuart
Doyle tells me to do. Like Uncle Edwin chose. Like he
went on to the end. Like he crawled out and dragged his
mates back. Bet he was pissing himself. Bet he was scared
– even more than I am.

21.30

> *U have have chosen*
> *The end is decided*
> *0600 Friday*
> *Kelling Park shelter*
> *Or have 2 make*
> *another appointment*
> *Don't forget the Smarties*
> *Check for instructions on the hour*

22.00
No messages

23.00
No messages

23.48
Shame it's got to end. Doyle said that. What's it mean?
But if I don't go, it won't ever end. My head's spinning
with questions. Going over and over the same stuff. Just
want it to finish.

Lying in the dark. I keep seeing Lester standing at the gate, looking up at me. Why didn't he wait for me? Why didn't he wait?

And suddenly I'm blubbing – shaking, eyes streaming, dribbling. Can't stop. I'm trying to keep it quiet – don't want anyone to hear. Blubbing into my pillow under my duvet. Not even sure who I'm crying for. Me? Lester? Both of us. Crying for all the time wasted. For all the crap that's happened.

Midnight
No messages.

I fetch my bag, find my pad and pen, and start to write. All the stuff that's happened to me since Monday. Then I write down the stuff that happened to Lester. Everything that I can remember – two years of stuff. I list the all the names.

Then I write another note. *I'm going to meet Stuart Doyle at 6 am at Kelling Park, Friday morning. If I'm not back when you get up – tell Mum.*

I'll leave it on my pillow. If I'm still upright, I'll be back before anyone gets up. If not, well they'll have to come and find me.

FRIDAY

05.10

I feel like I'm in a dream. Stupid pointless thoughts –
like, what shall I wear? Dark as night outside. Tiptoeing
around so as not to wake them up. I fold up the pages
from my pad and slide them under my T-shirts in the
drawer. *Don't think. Just go. Think of tomorrow. It'll be
over then. One way or another.*

05.55
Kelling Park shelter

He knows the right places. Out of the way. Out of sight.
Out of sound. One of those partitioned shelters with
seats on four sides so you can't see who's on the other
side. Can't see anyway – too dark. Turn off my torch.
Huddle into the corner of the seat. Feels like I'm the
only person alive. Eyes adjusting to the dark now. There's
a cobweb up there – all frosty, lit by the moon. Like I'm
seeing it with supernatural vision. Like it's blinking at
me. Every perfect line and drop and curve. Like it's made
of diamonds. How can a spider create a thing like that?
The wonder of it hits me. The moon looks like I could
touch it. The dark swallows me up. I'm disappearing –

being sucked out of myself – like I *could* leave my body and float. All at once this amazing feeling – of stillness, of vanishing. As if I can see the shelter from above – shrinking to a little dot. I feel calm – calm. Nothing can hurt me . . .

A sudden noise – and I'm zooming back to the real world. I can hear something. Someone's on the other side of the shelter. I can hear them moving about – must have come from a different direction. Is it Doyle?

Suddenly Doyle is standing in front of me. All wrapped up – scarf and hat. Beckons with his head for me to follow him to the other side.

'Ed? What're you doing here!' Ryan stands there – staring at me. He looks terrified. He looks at Doyle. 'But you said—'

'Shut up, Ryan,' says Doyle. 'Well? Where is it? Hurry up! I haven't got all day.'

Ryan tries to unzip his jacket. It gets stuck. His hands are shaking. He struggles – takes out a thick brown envelope and holds it out to Doyle.

'And the other one,' says Doyle, sliding the envelope inside his own jacket.

Ryan tugs out a plastic carrier bag. I recognise that bag.

'How much?' Doyle asks him.

'Dunno,' Ryan mumbles.

'Yes you do, Ryan. You told me last night, remember? Come on now – nice and clear. Tell your friend, Edwin here. How much?'

Ryan stares at the ground. 'One hundred and thirty-eight pounds fifty.'

Doyle starts to laugh. He's not putting it on. He's cracking up – like it's really funny. 'You know what this is, Edwin?' he manages to get out.

'It's the betting money.'

'Yeah,' he nods. 'Can you believe that? All those kids willing to bet on *you* Edwin! Betting on *you* beating me! On beating *anyone*! In some stupid fight? Well done, Ryan! Have to hand it to you – that was some nerve! You'll make a great con-man one day.' He shoves the bag inside his jacket.

Ryan looks like he's going to say something – then stops.

Doyle laughs. 'Sorry Ryan. I know I promised you could keep it – but the thing is, I need it more than you do. No hard feelings, eh?'

I stare at Ryan.

'Never thought you'd pull it off, Ryan,' smiles Doyle. 'But you did, didn't you? Congratulations!'

I look at Doyle's face with its smug smile – then at Ryan's scared white face. It sinks in what they're talking about.

'Who's idea was the betting, Ryan? Was it yours? Or his?'

'He made me do it, Ed!' he bleats. 'He *made* me!'

'You've got something else of mine, I believe?' Doyle

tells him. He holds out his hand.

'What?' Ryan croaks.

'The mobile, Ryan – the mobile!'

Now I see. I see how Doyle knew everything. It wasn't Ryan's sister's mobile – it was Doyle's. Ryan had sneaked. He'd been sneaking all the time. Ryan sees me looking at him.

'Look – I didn't have any choice, did I?' he whines.

'I'll have your mobile too, Edwin,' says Doyle. 'All right, Ryan – you can go now,' Doyle nods.

Ryan blinks with relief and turns to leave.

'No – on second thoughts, wait!' Doyle orders. He's smiling like he's just had an idea. Or maybe he's just enjoying tormenting Ryan. 'Now, Edwin. What about you, eh? What am I going to *do* with you?'

'Why ask me? I thought you were in charge of the game. I'm only a player, remember?' I can't believe I sound so calm. As if I'm two people standing here. The one whose legs feel boneless – who's quaking inside. And the one whose saying these words that are coming out of my mouth.

He smiles. 'Hope you brought the sweeties.'

I feel in my pocket for the Smarties tube and hold it out. He takes it, prises off the lid and pours something white and powdery into his hand. He licks his finger, dips it in, holds up his finger – it's coated with white.

'Want to know what this is?'

I shrug.

'What about you Ryan?'

Ryan says nothing.

'Come here, Ryan.'

Ryan nervously does as he's told. Doyle holds his finger up in front of Ryan's face.

'You're my guinea pig, Ryan. What can it be, eh? Lick it Ryan! Lick it for me!'

'What? What! No way! Don't know what it is, do I?'

'Come on Ryan! One tiny taste!'

Doyle presses his finger against Ryan's mouth. He's squirming.

'Don't make me! Don't make me!' Ryan's crying now.

Doyle laughs and licks his finger. 'Mmm,' he says. 'Icing sugar – that's all, Ryan. Icing sugar!'

'What?' says Ryan. 'You made me deliver a bag of sugar?'

Doyle smiles. 'Maybe, maybe not. You know something, Ryan. You are totally predictable.' He turns to me. 'Don't look so puzzled, Edwin. Remember – it's a game. So, how predictable are you, then? Did you do as I predicted, Edwin? Because if I win – so do you. Did we win the game or not?' He says, 'Remind me, Ryan. How much money did you take?'

Ryan wipes his nose on the back of his hand. 'One hundred and thirty-eight pounds fifty,' he sniffs.

'So, let's see. At odds of twenty to one, that makes two thousand, seven hundred and seventy quid – plus their stakes – makes – two thousand nine hundred and eight pounds fifty. So if boy noble Edwin here wins, looks like you're going to have to find a lot of cash, Ryan.'

Ryan stands hunched in his jacket, hands in pockets, staring down at the ground.

'Well, we'd better have that fight then. Wouldn't be fair on the punters, would it? Wouldn't be right. Taking money on false pretences, that is.'

I stare at him. Is he serious? I've lost then – I've lost. He thought I'd deliver. He thought I'd give in. Not so clever then, is he? And I'm glad! I'm glad I didn't give in!

'Ryan, you're the referee, right? Stand there!'

Ryan blinks at me open-mouthed, then at Doyle, and moves to where Doyle points.

'Come on, then, Edwin,' Doyle mocks. 'Come on!' He stands, half-crouched, legs apart, arms open, beckoning with his hands. 'Come on!'

'No.'

He laughs. 'But Edwin! This is your chance! Bet you've been dying to do this! Bet you've been imagining it. And what about all those techniques Elvira showed you, eh? What was it, Ryan? Surprise is your secret weapon? Come on, Edwin! Surprise me! Just imagine yourself telling everyone you beat me.'

He ambles slowly towards me, smirking. 'Look! I'll make it easy for you. I'll just stand here. I won't move! Come on! Hit me!'

He's standing right in front of me. Yeah. I'd love to hit

him! I'd love to kick him! But not when he *orders* me to. He's playing with me. There's something not right . . .

He lowers his arms. 'Tell me, Edwin, how's Jack?' He smiles.

'What?'

'My kid. Jack.' He's watching my face closely. 'You get my meaning, Edwin? Funny isn't it? That makes you my brother-in-law, well sort of. Does he take after me, my boy Jack? Ask your Ellie if she remembers the night of . . .'

I hit him! I hit him as hard as I can – but he moves and I hardly touch him! Yet – he's staggering back – bent over, clutching his gut, groaning.

Ryan stares at me – gobsmacked.

Then suddenly Doyle straightens up – smiling. 'Well,' he shrugs. 'Looks like you won, boy noble! You won!' he laughs. He turns and jogs off, disappears into the darkness.

06.35

Running. Running back home. Jack – Jack is Doyle's? Stuart Doyle – Jack's father! His father! How could she? How could she?

Car headlights – blinding me as I cross the road. Its horn honking at me. Screech of brakes behind me . . .

'Ed! Ed! Wait!'

I look over my shoulder. Mum? It's Mum's car! What's

she doing here! She's getting out – running towards me . . .

'Are you all right?' Mum's arms round me. 'Come on love. Come on – get in the car. It's OK, it's OK. Look! You're all wet! Oh, Ed!'

Hadn't noticed. Hadn't noticed it's raining.

07.25 Home

'Look! It's finished! I don't want to go over it all! You'll only make it worse! Anyway, it's sorted! Just leave it, Mum! Leave it!'

'I can't leave it, Ed.' She looks down at me. She's been crying. I can see that now. She puts a mug of hot chocolate on the table. I'm still shivering, even though I've had a hot shower.

'I found your note,' says Ellie. 'What does it mean? You've got to tell her, Ed.'

Mum takes my hands, looks into my face. 'This is really hard, Ed. It's why you have to tell us. You have to tell us everything. Everything that's been going on. Lester's dead, love. Lester's dead.'

THURSDAY

A week now since Lester killed himself. His mum found him when she got home from work. He was in the garage, sitting in the driving seat of a learner-driver car. He'd run a hose from the exhaust through the car window, then sealed the car up.

I keep seeing that. Can't get it out of my head.

Later, his mum found a letter he'd left – addressed to me. That's why she phoned Mum so early on Friday morning. When she brought the letter round, she told me Lester had talked to her about how he thought he might be gay – it was just after we split. Did he think that was that reason I went off with The Diehards – is that what he thought?

Lester's mum asked, '*If he could talk to me about that, why couldn't he tell me about the bullying, Ed? Why?*' She started crying then. So did I. Then she asked if I would say something at his funeral. What can I say? That I let him down?

She'd found a diary too. He'd kept a record of everything that happened to him. She'd started to read it, but couldn't bear it. There was lots about Doyle. The police have got it now.

■

Dad went back today. I'm going up to stay with him for a bit – after the funeral. He's building a wall in his garden and he wants me to help. He says it's good for getting your head sorted, building walls. And the doctor told Mum it'll do me good to get away.

Questions, so many questions. Everyone asking questions. Been having nightmares too, seeing terrible tortures, hearing screams – blood everywhere. Terrified of those dreams. Terrified, because it's *me* doing the tortures. Sometimes to Doyle, sometimes to Brett and the others. All of them.

Should have heard Ellie when I told her what Doyle said about Jack. '*God! You didn't believe him, Ed? Anyway, he doesn't fancy girls – it's boys he likes. Didn't you know that?*'

Did my head in, that. Never knew half of what Lester went through, did I? All that crap he got from Doyle. Can't think about it. Too heavy.

She says loads of people knew Doyle was involved in drugs. He didn't even hide it – used to boast that he could get anything. That's why the George Hotel was so popular.

■

The weird thing is that the inquest report said Lester

had been dead for hours when his mum found him. He died around three, four o'clock. But I keep telling them that I saw him at *six*. It *was* him! I *know* it was him! I didn't imagine it. I told Lester's mum – she was pleased I told her that. She wanted to know exactly how he looked, what he was wearing. Kept making me tell her.

Carl called round – lent me some videos and CDs. The joke is there are all these rumours going round at school that I won – that I beat Doyle in a big punch up. Who started that? Was it Doyle? It had to be – it wouldn't be Ryan. '*You won.*' That's what Doyle said – but *he* was laughing at me. I didn't even manage to hit him, did I?

I'm still trying to work Doyle out. Did he really know that I wouldn't make that delivery? And what was that stupid fake fight for? Deliberately taunting me – to make me lash out. What was it all about? Just to set Ryan up? To punish him for something? He must have really hated Ryan.

Carl hates Ryan for what he did – calls him the informer. It must have been Ryan who told Doyle about Elvira, and how they were able to follow Carl to Revolution Records. Even the betting was part of Doyle's game – playing us off against one another, then standing back and laughing. It wasn't a game – not to me. Not to Lester.

Kids keep asking Carl where Ryan is – they want their winnings. No one's seen him or heard from him. Carl says it's weird – everyone's talking about me like I *am* some sort of mini-hero. '*You did win,*' Carl said. '*In a way.*' Is this what winning feels like?

■

Caitlin says there's been a huge stink at school. Loads have been suspended – Zimmer, Sharples, Sonya and Brett's lot. Loads. Police in school as well, questioning kids. They came here too – going over it. Over and over.

There's been stuff in the papers and on the TV news about Lester – and the drugs. Oh, and Doyle's parents, pleading for news of him. He's disappeared, hasn't he? And I'm the last one to see him, apparently. Police have been round here again – more questions. Something must have happened for Doyle to take off like that. Maybe he planned it. Maybe he got in too deep with the drugs and decided to scarper. Maybe he just got bored. Didn't even take his car. Took his dad's credit cards though. One thing's for sure – Stuart Doyle will never be a loser.

Caitlin's been fantastic – she comes round every day. She says that what happened to Lester has shaken up kids really badly. So she and Meera organised a collection for a wreath – but they've had so many donations that they're going buy lots of wreaths. Then they had the idea of kids writing messages to Lester, and they're going to pin them on to the wreaths. Caitlin's asked Lester's mum if all the kids who've written messages can go to the funeral and read them out, to show that not all kids are like Doyle and Sonya and Brett and the rest. And that's what's going to happen.

I'm going to say something about Lester at the funeral, too. '*Tell them that story you told me, Ed – the one about the car ride,*' Caitlin said. 'That was the *real* Lester.' Don't know what I'd do without Caitlin. I can talk to her like no one else.

■

When Lester's mum gave me his letter, I could see from her face that she was desperate to know what he'd written. I didn't want to open it – I was really nervous. But I did.

Thanks Ed.
Sorry
Quitters One.

Started blubbing again didn't I? Couldn't stop. Mum says it's OK to cry. I should cry all I want.

Lester's mum asked, '*What does it mean? Quitters one? What does it mean, Ed?*'

I tried to explain. See, when we'd just moved up from Cubs to Scouts, we had this really feeble Scout leader,

Brian. He was useless. Week after week it was totally boring. He was always promising exciting stuff, like raft-building, a treasure hunt or tracking – but they never happened. He'd forget or change his mind – and when we complained he'd lose his temper and we'd end up doing knots or something. If we moaned he'd start ranting on and on, '*Winners never quit and quitters never win.*'

Then one particularly boring evening it really got to Lester. He jumped up, threw down his knots, and announced, 'Right! That's it! I quit! I'm never gonna waste time on stupid pointless stuff again! I quit! Proud to quit!' He was waving his arms in the air like a champion. 'Proud to be a quitter!'

Kids started joining in, marching round the hall, chanting, '*Proud to quit! Proud to quit! Proud to be a quitter!*'

Man, it was so funny. Everyone laughing, old Brian doing his nut – and no one taking any notice of him. Afterwards, me and Lester, we formed our own two-member secret society. Quitters United – motto: *Never waste time on stupid pointless stuff.*

■

The Wall of Death. Think I understand that now – what it was all about. It was a test, wasn't it? For Lester, it was to prove he wasn't scared – of Matt, The Diehards or

The Wall. To stand up to all that piss-taking. And then he walked away. He was waiting for me to join him – but I didn't. He was giving me a choice – him or The Diehards. I couldn't see that. I was too stupid – and too angry with him for what he put me through making that climb. So, he pedalled off. For days I waited, hoping he'd turn up. It wasn't him that let *me* down. It was the other way round. Reckon we were both waiting for the other one to turn up.

■

Mr Grimshaw came to see me too. He wants to know why I didn't tell anyone what was happening. Doesn't have a clue, does he?

But if I had to go through it again? If I had to watch Lester being tormented, seeing him getting all that shit? Yeah – I'll dob! I'll grass! I'll be *proud* to be a dobber! I'll dob to the world! I'll even wear a badge! DOBBERS UNITED! I'll organise a whole army of dobbers!

■

I *know* I didn't imagine it. It *was* Lester. He was standing at the gate – as real as anything. He'd come to say goodbye, hadn't he? He looked happy. Really happy – like the old days. Like I hadn't seen him in ages. It's all right. He's OK. He's flying over mountains peaks.

Riding an iceberg. Travelling on his own astral plane. A free spirit now. No problemo.

A note from the author

The idea for this story
was planted years ago when
my son read *THE EIGHTEENTH
EMERGENCY*, by Betsy Byars. It's one
of my favourite books — about a boy who
knows that the school hardcase is out to get him.
My son loved it — but added, 'In real life bullies
are nastier — and the stories don't always have
happy endings. You should write a story like that.'

This is that story. Some of it came from my
imagination. Some of it really happened.

Pat Moon is the author of many books
for children, including *BARKING MAD*
and *DO NOT READ THIS BOOK*.

BLUE

Sue Mayfield

'You've lost weight . . . mind you don't get anorexic,'
Hayley said, sounding concerned. 'You're all skin and
bone!' She glanced sideways at Ruth Smith, and they
smiled conspiratorially.

'Anna-rexic!' said Ruth with a snort of laughter . . .

When Hayley, the most popular girl at school,
wants to be her best mate, new girl Anna
Goldsmith can't believe her luck. Charismatic
and confident, Hayley Parkin is definitely
someone to be in with – who *wouldn't* want to be
her friend?!

But this friendship comes at a price. Because
Hayley enjoys playing games. Spiteful, vicious
and dangerous games . . .

MAGENTA ORANGE

Echo Freer

Magenta Orange has the world at her feet. If she could just stop tripping over them . . .

Bright, sassy and massively accident-prone, Magenta is seen as a bit of a jinx by her mates – and a positive disaster-zone by the boy of her dreams!

Blind to the longing looks of her best friend, Daniel, oblivious to the sweet-nothings of the school geek, Spud, Magenta has set her sights on Year Eleven babe-magnet, Adam Jordan.

And she will risk anything, even total public humiliation, in her relentless pursuit of a date . . .

ORDER FORM

Also available in the 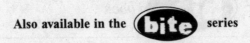 series

0 340 81732 1	Nostradamus and Instant Noodles	£4.99	❏
	John Larkin		
0 340 81746 1	Festival	£4.99	❏
	David Belbin		
0 340 81762 3	Speak	£4.99	❏
	Laurie Halse Anderson		
0 340 80519 6	Blue	£4.99	❏
	Sue Mayfield		
0 340 84148 6	Magenta Orange	£4.99	❏
	Echo Freer		

All Hodder Children's books are available at your local bookshop, or can be ordered direct from the publisher. Just tick the titles you would like and complete the details below. Prices and availability are subject to change without prior notice.

Please enclose a cheque or postal order made payable to *Bookpoint Ltd*, and send to: Hodder Children's Books, 130 Milton Park, Abingdon, OXON OX14 4SB, UK. Email Address: orders@bookpoint.co.uk

If you would prefer to pay by credit card, our call centre team would be delighted to take your order by telephone. Our direct line *01235 400414* (lines open 9.00 am–6.00 pm Monday to Saturday, 24 hour message answering service). Alternatively you can send a fax on *01235 400454*.

TITLE		FIRST NAME		SURNAME	

ADDRESS	

DAYTIME TEL:		POST CODE	

If you would prefer to pay by credit card, please complete:
Please debit my Visa/Access/Diner's Card/American Express (delete as applicable) card no:

Signature .... Expiry Date: ....

If you would NOT like to receive further information on our products please tick the box. ❏